Voice

of

Tears

Christian S. Branch

Printed in the United States of America.
ISBN: 979-8-9862546-0-9
First Printing, 2022
Little Rock, AR 72209

To all the voices
that have been silenced for generations...

Chapter One

A s I turn into the parking lot at 12 Safe Haven Boulevard, I answer my ringing cell phone.

"Hello?"

"You're late! Church doesn't start until noon, so why are you always late?" my sister gripes.

"I know. I know," I reply.

"Are you on the way?"

"Yes, Charity. I'm about to turn into the parking lot now."

"I'll see you in a few minutes," she says and quickly ends the call.

I join the line of cars that arrived moments before I did. While I wait for traffic to flow, I admire the scenery at the church. A sign with "Beautifully Blessed Christian Church" flashing in gold letters with a white background is displayed in the grass to the left. White security booths are near the front and rear entrances of the parking lot. The lawn is neatly manicured, and a beautiful flowerbed adds just enough color to the area near the entrance to the church. The security guard, Thomas, waves as I drive past his booth. As I look around for a parking spot, I

1

notice Jonathan Peersyn, also known as JP, walking towards me.

"Would you like for me to park your car, Mr. Fox?" he asks as I stop next to him.

"No thanks, JP. Here you go."

I grab ten dollars from the console and hand it to him for offering.

"Thank you, Mr. Fox."

"You're welcome."

I locate a spot in the rear of the lot and park. As I get out of the car, I take a moment to marvel at the beautiful spring day. White clouds are dancing across the blue sky. As I walk towards the two-story white building, I admire the manicured rose beds that surround the entrance to the church. I walk up the gold staircase through the double glass door entrance into the foyer. The area is enclosed in white walls with gold trim at the top and bottom. The Information Center, located to the left side of the entrance, showcases pamphlets regarding the Sunday services, Wednesday night bible study, childcare and nursery, and various ministries. A plush white couch and chairs with lavender accent pillows beautifies the right side of the entrance. Straight ahead, the white doors to the sanctuary are already open. I made it just in time for fellowship hour.

Fellowship hour… meet…greet…and hugging. This isn't my favorite part of service. I have never been a fan of having people in my personal space. That's way too much touching for me. I look around at the light lavender walls with white trim around the base. The sanctuary and choir stand are filled with whitewashed wood pews that are seated atop lavender carpet. The accent wall in front of the choir stand is white with gold trim at the base. Gold chandeliers illuminate the ceilings. The choir members are wearing their white robes with a gold cross emblem on the front. As I walk towards my seat, the congregation has already risen to visit one another. There are so many smiling faces on people dressed in their Sunday best. Deacon Hopkins makes his way towards me with his hand extended.

"Good morning, Bro. Jaxxson."

I return the gesture by extending my hand with a firm handshake. "Good morning, Deacon Hopkins. How are you doing?"

"Oh, I am blessed and highly favored in the house of the Lord! How are you?"

"Amen. I'm good."

"Good to see you, Brother."

"Good to see you, too, Deacon."

As Deacon Hopkins eases over to Sis. Dot, I spot my sister, Charity, talking to Celine Brown. Charity is a 5'3" dark brown skinned, slim young lady with light brown eyes. I overhear Celine compliment her on her new haircut, a shoulder-length bob, as I continue walking towards my seat. Next, I spot my gorgeous mother ending a conversation with Mother Jacobs. My mother, Desirae Fox, is a 5' light skinned petite lady with long curly black hair and light brown eyes. As I get closer to my seat, Mother Hensley stops me.

"Good morning, Mother Hensley. How are you feeling?"

"Hi, Jaxxson. I haven't been feeling too well. I have been having some problems with my legs and feet swelling for about a week. My blood pressure has been running a little high lately. And, I just got over a cold, but I can't shake this hacking cough. I have an appointment with Dr. Cameron tomorrow."

"Yes, ma'am. I hope that you get to feeling better soon, Mother Hensley," I say as I hurriedly walk away. Finally, I make it to my seat next to Pops. Germaine Fox, is a 6'4" dark brown skinned man with an athletic build, curly gray hair, and hazel eyes.

"Good morning, Pops."

"Good morning, son," he replies as my mother returns to her seat.

"Hi sweetie!" she says as soon as she spots me.

"Hi Mama."

Charity says, "Running late again," and takes a seat next to Mama.

"I missed you too, sis!"

She playfully sticks her tongue out at me and then we face the pulpit and wait for service to begin. We have attended Beautifully Blessed Christian Church with Pastor Grace and First Lady Laiyah Grace for years. I remember Mama was at her wits end with my behavior problems growing up. She talked to Pastor Grace about getting help to get me back on track.

"Pastor Grace, I just don't know what else I can do to help Jaxxson control his anger. He constantly gets into trouble at school - mostly fighting. I can't keep a job because he keeps getting suspended. And, I can't get a new one until he is settled. He attends therapy sessions weekly, but that doesn't seem to help. His father hasn't been in the picture for two years. I love my son, but I am exhausted. Everything has been on my shoulders for years," she cried one day in his office.

"Desirae, maybe Jaxxson needs a different approach."

"What type of approach, Pastor?"

"I think he needs some consistent positive male influences," our pastor said calmly.

"I agree. I've tried to get help from the men in my family, but that didn't work out so well. They're usually too busy. Or, they say they will come get him but never show up. Half of the time, they're dodging my calls. So, I stopped reaching out to them. I've done everything that I know to help him. I have been on the verge of a meltdown for a while. I really can't afford to have a mental breakdown. I already don't have the help that I need. If I break down, who will take care of Jaxxson and Charity?" Mama began to shed more tears. "I am exhausted, Pastor!"

"I'm sorry that your family and his father haven't been helpful. I definitely don't want you to have a mental breakdown." Pastor Grace hands Mama his handkerchief. "I may have a solution for help with Jaxxson."

"What do you have in mind?"

"We have a member, Germaine Fox, who founded the Building Better Men Program. It's a mentoring program for young men who have similar behavior problems. He has helped some of the other children within the community. Maybe, he can help you with Jaxxson. I can give you his contact information. And, I can talk to him as well."

"That would be great, Pastor…"

After Mama connected with the program coordinator, they got me enrolled, and it made a tremendous difference in my life. She and Germaine Fox eventually start dating and get married. He even adopted my sister and me. And, our lives finally saw some happiness.

I return my focus to the pulpit as everyone returns to their seats. Moments later, the ushers' gesture for the congregation to stand for the reading of God's word. Pastor Grace is already at the podium.

He says, "If you have your bibles, turn to Colossians 3:13 NIV. If you don't, just look at the screen above you. 'Bear with each other and forgive one another if any of you has a grievance against someone. Forgive as the Lord forgave you.' Today's message: It's time to let go of all the hurt and forgive. Forgive and forget. You may be seated. I won't be before you long."

Echoes of "Amen" ring throughout the sanctuary as everyone disperses to their seats.

"As most of you already know, about twenty years ago, I made the biggest mistake of my life. I was a man of God… but… the temptation of the flesh was stronger. I had a brief affair with one of my church members - Celeste."

The congregation gasps.

"During that time, we were attending Heavenly Haven Christian Church. Celeste was an attractive 4'5" shapely figured woman with smooth caramel skin. She was always willing to lend a helping hand by feeding the homeless, fundraising, traveling with the church, etc. Whatever needed to be done, she was ready to jump in and help."

Pastor notices all the surprised looks on everyone's faces.

He glances toward First Lady and says, "we have already discussed this matter. It's not her favorite topic. The Lord said it's time for me to help someone in a similar situation." He begins to recall his affair with Celeste. "Celeste and I would get together at every possible moment when traveling out of town. As you know…. what's done in the dark will surely come to the light!"

"Yes, Lord! Amen, Pastor Grace," responds the congregation.

He continues, "Naturally, rumors were circulating throughout the church. In fact, that's how she found out. Not because I told her… Not because Celeste told her… There were rumors within the church."

7

More gasps come from the congregation.

"I had just returned home from a conference in Missouri. I walked into our home and heard Laiyah crying. Now, ladies and gentlemen... My wife is a very strong woman. It takes a lot for her to break down and cry. I knew this was something major. My first thought was something happened to our son or parents. So, I dropped everything and ran over to her. Baby, what's wrong? She responded, 'How could you?' 'How could I what?' I asked. You see, I had no idea what she knew. So, she enlightened me.

"She said, 'How could you cheat on me? I have been nothing but a good woman... wife to you... mother to our son... woman of God! Why? It's all around the church about you and Celeste!'"

Pastor pauses for a moment and tries to contain his emotions. "I immediately say, 'I'm so sorry, Laiyah! I made a terrible mistake!' 'You are only sorry because I'm saying something about it! You just left her, didn't you?' I opened my mouth to speak, but nothing came out. Laiyah got up and left the room... Ladies and gentlemen, I was at a loss for words. In my mind, she didn't have a clue about the affair. However, there was so much pain in her eyes... in her words. I made a fool out of myself! But, I made an even bigger fool out of my wife!

"I'm supposed to be a man of God... but... my actions didn't reflect it. I never planned to be the type of man who cheats on his wife. How could I counsel married couples while cheating on my wife? How could I preach God's word while allowing the devil into my life? I was a hypocrite! At that moment, I fell on my knees and began to cry out to the Lord. I had to repent and ask for forgiveness!

"I broke it off with Celeste and then I stepped away from counseling couples and preaching for a while. My wife and I began marriage counseling with a professional therapist. There were moments when she was ready to forgive me. And, there were moments of anger and frustration. I betrayed her trust. She didn't want anything to do with me. I tried sending flowers, candy, jewelry, and more. Nothing worked! It was like she had an electric fence up protecting her heart. And, it seemed like nothing was penetrating that fence. She did a lot of crying, screaming, and praying! It took a long, long time to regain her trust. When I finally did, I placed my focus back on God and my family. And, I never looked back! Now, we are stronger than ever!" he says as he looks at his wife and smiles. She returns the sentiment.

"Of course, it was not an easy journey to forgiveness. I will never jeopardize her heart again. Forgive and forget. We all make mistakes, and we all deserve forgiveness. Now, this does not give you the right to keep making the same mistakes repeatedly. Some of you have been in similar situations. Some of you have been in worse situations. You came in with the weight of the world on your shoulders. Well, it's time to let go of all the hurt and forgive. Forgive and forget. The doors of the church are now open as the altar workers are coming. If you need prayer, come! If you need a church home, come! It's time to forgive and forget."

As I listen to Pastor Grace's message, a sadness covers me. *Forgive and forget.* Those are two words that I have had the hardest time doing lately. How do I forgive and forget? Where do I start? Why do I have to forgive and forget? I didn't do anything wrong. I was only a child. He turned his back on me!

Pops leans over and whispers to me, "Are you okay?"

"I'm fine," I say with a smile.

"Are you sure?"

"Yes sir…" I repeat as I think about my life.

My world is perfect. I was promoted to Engineer Technician approximately six months ago after earning my Bachelor of Science in Engineering degree from Higher Achievement University. I'm a 6'3" single man with an athletic build. I have dark brown skin, brown eyes, a goatee, and a low-cut black fade with waves. I have no baby mama drama. I'm drug and alcohol free. I own my home and vehicle. I go to church and tithe regularly. I'm a mentor at my father's Building Better Men Program. Overall, I'm a good person.

Well, everything was great until my world changed three months ago with the arrest of my father - my biological father - Jayyson Craig. He was arrested and charged with first degree murder in the death of his wife, Jada Craig. *Jayyson Craig*. I haven't seen or talked to him since I was nine years old. Fourteen years! Wow, it's been fourteen years! Forgive and forget! Yeah, that sounds good, but I am definitely not there yet. As I think back on my relationship - or lack thereof - with my father, my thoughts are interrupted with cheers of "Amen." Members and visitors are walking away from the altar with tears in their eyes after receiving prayer.

Pastor Grace asks, "Will there be another? Forgive and forget. None of us are perfect! Come judgement day, we all have to account for our sins!"

No one else walks to the altar.

"Lord, we have done what you have asked us to do. Thank you, altar workers. Everyone, please rise for the benediction… Gracious Father, we need your help! We have all done something that we need to be granted forgiveness for. And, we have all had something done to us that we need to give forgiveness. Open our hearts, Lord! Open our minds! It's time for us to release all the hurt, anger, frustration, disappointment, and bitterness. Release all the negative energy that has consumed us for so long. Release it so that we can move forward! Keep us safe as we travel to our various destinations. These and other blessings, Lord! Amen."

"Amen" rings throughout the sanctuary as the congregation dissipates and says their final goodbyes to one another. I head to my parents' home for Sunday dinner.

Chapter Two

Sunday dinners have always been a tradition for us to ensure that we are spending time together as a family. Before church, mama made smothered pork chops, baked macaroni and cheese, candied yams, greens, cornbread, and peach cobbler for dessert. As soon as we get to their house from church, we wash up and sit down at the dinner table. Pops says grace.

"Dear Heavenly Father, thank you for the nourishments you have provided to our minds, bodies, and souls. Thank you for blessing us with such a wonderful family. Please continue to guide us according to Your plan. Please continue to remove any negativity and roadblocks from within our pathways. These and other blessings we pray. Amen."

We all say, "Amen," and Pops starts the conversation as we begin to take bites of our food.

"So, what did everyone think of today's message?"

Mama responds, "It was a really good message. Forgiveness is just hard to do."

Charity chimes in, "Yes, it is."

Pops says, "Forgive as the Lord forgave you. Pastor is right. We have all sinned just in different ways." He turns to me and says, "Jaxx, I can tell that message hit you pretty hard."

"Yeah, it did. I was just a child… I didn't do anything wrong. He left us."

"I know, son, but you must forgive. Forgiveness is not for him; it is for you," Pops says.

"So, you think I should go to see him?"

"Yes, I do. It definitely won't be easy. But, you should at least hear him out."

I think about it for a second. I know Pops is right, but I'm not sure if I'm ready. "I don't know! I will think about it."

"Pray about it. Ask the Lord for His guidance."

"I will, Pops," I say as I stand up and take my plate in the kitchen to empty it.

Mama follows me, "Jaxxson, you barely touched your food."

"I guess I'm just not that hungry."

"Sweetie, I know the news about Jayyson is weighing heavily on you. Don't let it stress you out. You didn't do anything wrong. Just continue to pray about it."

My mom pulls me into an embrace. I hug her back.

"I will, Mama. I'm going to head home."

"Are you sure?"

"I'm sure. Thank you for dinner."

"You are welcome, sweetie,"

I walk out the kitchen and stop by the dinner table. "Pops, I'm headed home."

"Be careful. And, remember what I said, Jaxx."

"Yes sir. Bye, Charity," I say as I playfully tap my sister on the head.

"Bye, Jaxx."

I let everybody know that I love them as I'm headed out the door. Then, I ride home in silence as I usually do. Except this time, the silence is too loud. They say an idle mind is the devil's playground. Well, the devil has been having a field day with my mind lately. Every time I turn on the news or radio I hear, *"Jayyson Craig tortured and killed wife, Jada Craig."* There's nowhere to turn without being reminded of my father and his evil wife. As I pull into my garage, I wonder what finally pushed Jayyson over the edge to kill Jada. What did she do that made him feel that killing her was the only solution? The phone rings, as I walk into my home. `Unknown caller` displays across the screen. I wonder who this could be. I'm hesitant but I answer.

"Hello?"

"You have a call from inmate 67845-BR. Will you accept the charges?" an automated voice says.

I pause for a moment before responding. "Yes. Hello?"

"Hey, son."

After locking the door, I walk over to the couch and have a seat.

"Jayyson?"

"Yeah. How have you been Jaxxson?"

"No, you don't get to do that! It's been fourteen years! Don't pretend to care about me now!" I yell.

I feel all the anger, pain, and sadness inside me come to a boiling point.

"You're right. I'm sorry that is has been so long," he replies calmly.

I manage to calm myself down and try to control my emotions. "What do you want, Jayyson?"

"I want to see you. I want a chance to explain."

"And, what makes you think that I want to hear anything you have to say?"

"Please, son! I know you're very angry with me. And, you have every right to be. Just give me a chance to explain," he pleads.

"I'll think about it. Goodbye, Jayyson." *Click* The nerve of him! Why would I want to hear anything that he has to say? He could have explained fourteen years ago! He turned his back on Mama, Charity, and me! Why reach out now? And, how did he know I was just thinking about him? I begin walking towards my bedroom. Oh, *that's* it! He just wants to clear his conscience. Yep, that's all he is doing.

What about the damage that he did by not believing me? Not to mention, the damage his nasty wife did to me. It took a lot of work to get to where I am today. There were moments when I felt so ashamed, thinking I did something wrong. There were so many days when I was filled with so much hate and anger that I didn't know how to control it. Days that I kept reliving the trauma and I hated my life.... I don't even want to think about all the hell that Mama went through with me.

Man, I know there were days that she wanted to give up on me. Thankfully, she never did! But, Jayyson... Oh, he got rid of me the first chance he didn't hear what he wanted to hear. What kind of man gives up on his child? Love is supposed to be unconditional. Conditional love is not an option! But, that's what he had for me. His love was unconditional as long as there was no problem. And, the moment there was a problem, it switched to conditional. Who does that? He didn't even take the time to consider the possibility that his wife was a child molester! Why would I lie about some shit like that? Now, he wants to explain. What is there to explain? You turned your back on me!

My rants are interrupted as the phone rings. "Hello?"

"Jaxxson, did I wake you?"

"No, Charity. What's up?"

"Did Jayyson call you?"

"How'd you know?" I ask.

"He called me earlier."

"Oh."

"He wants to see us."

"Well, I don't want to see him!" I state firmly.

"I don't want to see him either, but I think we need to go," she says.

"Why?"

"Time to forgive."

"That's easy for you to say, Charity!"

She sighs and continues, "Jaxxson, I know all the work it took for you to get on track. Remember, I was there with you."

"I'm sorry, Charity. I didn't mean to snap at you. I just don't think I'm ready to see him."

"Well, I don't think we will ever be ready to see him… but, we can at least hear him out."

I consider her stance. "Yeah, I know. I just need some time to think about it. This is a lot to handle!"

"I understand. Take all the time you need to think about it. I was thinking about going to see him in a few weeks," she says.

"I will let you know."

"I love you, Jaxx."

"I love you too, Charity."

We hang up, and the heaviness remains on me.

"Lord, please help me. What am I supposed to do? There was so much hurt and pain. I overcame a lot with Your help…the help of Mama, Charity, and Pops. No help from Jayyson! None! He didn't even believe me! I was nine years old. Why would he think I made it up? Why would anybody make that up? I didn't know anything about sex before Jada! Jayyson didn't even consider the possibility that I might be telling the truth. Of course, I was telling the truth! Lord, please help me! Nine years old…" I cry out.

I lie on my bed and begin to daydream. My thoughts drift...

"I want my Mama," I said in a frightened tone as tears streamed down my cheeks.

"Your Mama ain't here!" Jada shouted.

"I want my daddy."

"Daddy, ain't here either! It's just you and me!" I cried more.

"Jaxxson, shut up!" she said.

I sniffled as I try to hold back my tears.

"Your Mama don't want you! She's tired of you being around. Why do you think you're over here? And, your daddy... I have him wrapped around my fingers. He won't believe anything you say against me. This is my family! I can do whatever I want to you, and there is nothing that you can do about it! Now, put your clothes on and go watch TV."

Daddy walked in, and Jada kissed him and said, "Hey baby!"

I came running into the living room. "Daddy! Daddy! I want to go home to Mama! I can't stay here anymore!"

"Why do you want to go home, Jaxxson?" he asked.

"Jada is mean! She hurts me every time you leave for work until right before you come home. She makes me do stuff that I don't want to do."

"Hurt you, how?" He laughed and asked, "Did she make you clean your room?"

"No... She..."

Jada shot an evil glare at me. I froze.

"What happened, Jaxxson?" my daddy asked.

"She...She...She bit me in my private area. She made me kiss her, and it tasted nasty. She put her finger in my bottom. And, she was on top of me. I told her to stop, but she wouldn't. I told her it hurt, but she didn't care," I finally said.

"Jaxxson! Jada wouldn't do no shit like that!" my dad fussed.

Jada stood behind him smiling and mouthing, "I told you."

"Daddy, I'm telling the truth! She is a bad person!"

Jada screamed, "Jayyson, he's lying! He took off walking, again. I told him that you would whoop him after I told you. He started yelling and cursing me out."

"Daddy, she is lying! Jada is a really bad person!"

"Stop lying!" he said.

As tears rolled down my cheeks, I yelled, "Daddy, I'm telling the truth!"

"Jada wouldn't do that!" he yelled back.

I couldn't believe my ears. "But daddy..."

"Stop it, Jaxxson! Go pack your bags! I'm taking you home!"

He called Mama as I headed to my room to gather my belongings. "Desirae! I have you on speaker phone!"

"Why are you yelling, Jayyson?"

"I'm bringing Jaxxson home! I can't do this anymore!"

"You can't do what? You have only had him for two weeks. What happened?" my mom asked.

19

"He took off walking, again. He was talking back to Jada. He yelled at her and cursed her out."

"Jayyson, what did she do to him?"

"What do you mean?"

"Jaxxson takes off walking when he is upset about something major. So, what did your wife do to my son?"

"She didn't do anything to him…"

My dream is interrupted by the sound of my alarm. I raise up to turn off the alarm and glance at the time. 6:00 a.m. Great! I just went to sleep a few hours ago. I try to get out of bed, but my head is pounding. It feels like I have a major hangover. I know that's not the case because I haven't had a drop of alcohol in years. Ouch! My head is throbbing. I lay back down because I can't go to work like this. I begin to search around in my bed and check my nightstand for my phone. Oh, here it is. I call Mr. Jessup at the office.

"Good morning, Mr. Jessup. I'm sorry it's so early. Unfortunately, I'm not feeling well… Yeah, I think it's just a stomach bug. I'm going to take a few sick days to be on the safe side…Yes sir! Thanks again, Mr. Jessup! Goodbye…"

I end the call and grab some pain medicine and water from the nightstand. I take three pills and drift back to sleep…

"Daddy didn't believe me. Why didn't he believe me, Mama?"

"I don't know, Jaxx. We're not going to worry about daddy. God will handle him! We have to focus on you! You can't keep getting into fights at school. This is your second time getting suspended, and it's only the first month of school. I can't keep losing jobs."

"I'm sorry, Mama. Alex made me so mad that I couldn't help it."

"Jaxxson, we have to get your anger under control. What happened to using the coping skills that you learned in therapy?"

"I know. When I'm upset, those coping skills go out the window."

"You have to control your anger. If you don't, you could end up in some trouble that no one can help you out of…not even Mama."

"I'm trying; I'm sorry."

"I know you are sweetheart! We will work on it together!"

"Thank you, Mama!"

"You're welcome!"

"Mama?"

"Yes, son."

"Can we have a movie night?"

She laughed and said, "Sure…"

Chapter Three

I wake up smiling and my headache is gone. I remember the last part of dream and think movie night sounds good. I decide to visit Pops and Mama. I get up and do my normal routine of getting ready for the day. Then, I grab my keys and head out the door. I ride in silence with memories of movie nights with Mama and Charity playing in my head. Mama would always let Charity and me take turns picking the movie. We usually had buffalo mild wings with ranch dressing, pizza, and a soda. Of course, we had dessert - ice cream, cake, cookies, or cinnamon rolls. Basically, a movie and junk food... And, when Mama married Pops, we had movie nights with him as well. Those were some good times!

My thoughts switch to Pops and how much his program helped me. I reroute and head to his office. He used one of the old middle schools for the Building Better Men program. I pull up to the building and see a mural of Pops and the volunteers that I painted when I was thirteen years old. Surprisingly, through the program in art therapy, I discovered that I have a talent for drawing. Art therapy was my favorite class. It helped me work through my emotions and develop self-awareness. I wanted to express my appreciation for all the help that I received from the workers and figured the mural was a great way to do it. Everyone loved it! Sometimes, I still volunteer to teach the art class. When I walk into the building, I go straight to his office.

"Jaxxson, this is a pleasant surprise," he says with a smile.

"Hi, Pops!"

"Aren't you supposed to be at work?" he quizzes.

I took a few days off.

"What's wrong, son?"

"Why do you think something is wrong?"

"Because you never take off work!"

I laugh and reply, "Yeah, that's true. I just have a lot on my mind."

"Have a seat. Talk to me," he says as he gives me his undivided attention.

Well, I started having those dreams again. You know, the ones with Jada and Jayyson…"

"I see. How long has this been going on?"

"On and off since Jayyson's arrest. And, he called me last night.

"Really? Why?"

"Yeah. He says he wants to explain."

"What did you say?" he asks.

"I told him that I would think about it, and then I hung up."

"So, what are your thoughts about it?"

"I'm angry! It's been fourteen years! He never thought to reach out in fourteen years. Why reach out now? He turned his back on Mama, Charity, and me. We dealt with so much pain, suffering, and anger over the years! It took a long time for me to get to this point. He didn't do anything to help me when I needed it. Why does he want to see me now? He didn't believe me, Pops! My own father didn't believe me! I don't want anything to do with him!" I yell.

"Jaxxson, I am not going to say that your feelings aren't valid. You have every right to feel the way you do. I didn't come into your life until you were eleven years old. You were an extremely angry child. You didn't know how to deal with all the emotions you were feeling. You were constantly acting out in school having fights, talking back to the teachers, walking out of class, walking out of school, multiple suspensions and expulsions and more.

"The security guards knew you were involved every time they got a call for assistance. Desirae and I worked hard to help turn around your behavior. I know what you have been through, Jaxx. I saw your constant struggles with working through the trauma. You had to overcome a lot at such a young age. As a father, Jayyson should not have turned his back on you. And, as much as you don't want to see him, I do think you need to go."

"Why?" I ask.

"Because you have a lot of unanswered questions... Like it or not, Jayyson is the one person that can answer them. It's time to forgive! You can't continue to hold on to that hurt and anger. It will destroy you."

"Forgive? I didn't do anything wrong. I was a child!"

"You're right! You were a child and didn't do anything wrong in that situation. You're a grown man now. It's time for you to forgive! Forgiveness is for you. It's not for the other person. That's the only way that you will finally be healed from it. I'm not saying that seeing him will instantly erase all of the anger you feel towards him. It will definitely take some time, but you have to start somewhere…baby steps. Hear the man out," Pops pleads.

"I don't know, Pops. Charity wants to go see him in a few weeks."

"That would be great! Charity can help keep you calm," he laughs.

"Yes, she can." I laugh, too. "I'll think about it. Thanks, Pops!"

"Anytime, Jaxx!"

"No, I mean it. Thank you for everything that you did for me growing up. I know I wasn't the easiest person to deal with back then. You could have easily washed your hands with me a long time ago, but you didn't. You refused to give up on me even when I tried to give up on myself. You taught me how to persevere through life's challenges. Just because I had some bad things happen in my childhood, that doesn't define the rest of my life. Thank you for being my father!"

"You are welcome, son. That means a lot to me."

We embrace in a hug. "I think I'll head out."

"Alright. Where are you headed?"

"I was thinking of surprising Mama and taking her to lunch," I say.

"That would be great! She would love that. I love you, Jaxx."

"I love you too, Pops!" We embrace in another hug, and I leave.

My mom works at Ernie's Telecommunications which is not far from the program. She's worked there for twelve years as the Human Resources Director. She started out at the bottom and worked her way up to the top. This was the only company that worked with her when it came to my behavior issues. As I enter the building, I think about the number of times she had to take off to pick me up from school yet again.

"Good afternoon, Jaxxson. How are you doing today?"

"Hello, Max. I'm good. How are things in the world of security?"

"Same ole, same ole. Are you here to see your mom?" he asks.

"Yes sir."

"One moment." He lifts the phone receiver. "Mrs. Fox, Jaxxson is here to see you…Yes ma'am." He hangs up the phone receiver. "You can head up to her office."

"Thanks." I take the elevators up to the fourth floor. Her office is the first one to the right as I step off the elevators. I knock on the door.

"Come in," Mama says.

I open the door and walk in. Mama walks over and hugs me.

"This is a pleasant surprise. To what do I owe this visit?"

"I just thought that it would be nice to surprise you and take you to lunch."

"Oh really?" She folds her arms in disbelief.

"Yes, ma'am."

"So, where are you taking me?"

"I was thinking the Red Bottom Galore Restaurant downtown."

"That's a good choice." She unfolds her arms after reassurance.

"Shall we?" I ask as I extend my arm to escort her.

"We shall," she says as she interlocks her arm into mine.

We walk out to my car. I open the door and wait for her to get seated before I close it. I take my seat next to her and begin driving towards our destination…

"Jaxxson?"

"Yes ma'am."

"Why aren't you at work? Did something happen?" she asks.

"No, ma'am. I just needed a couple days to clear my head. I just left from seeing Pops. We talked for a little bit. Then, I thought it would be nice to take my wonderful mother to lunch."

"That's sweet! So, what's on your mind?"

"Well...I started having those dreams again. And...Jayyson called me last night."

"I see. Are you sleeping?"

"Not really," I confess.

"What did Jayyson say?"

"He wants a chance to explain. But, there's really nothing left for him to explain. He abandoned us and chose a woman he barely knew over his family. Now, he just wants to clear his conscience. Charity wants us to go visit him in a few weeks. I'm not sure that's a good idea though," I say as I find a parking spot at the restaurant.

I get out and escort Mama to the front door. Red Bottom Galore Restaurant is a black building with its name flashing in red lights. After walking through the glass double doors, we are greeted by the hostess standing behind the black podium."

"How many?" she asks.

"Two."

"Right this way."

As we walk to our table, we're surrounded by multiple waitresses dressed in their standard

28

uniforms that consist of a black long-sleeved button-down blouse, black skirt, red tie, and black red-bottom heels. The hostess directs us to a table near the bar. We have a seat.

"My name is Gabriella. I will be your waitress this afternoon. What can I get you to drink?" she says.

Mama responds, "I'll have water with lemon."

"I'll have water but no lemon," I add.

"Alright. I'll give you a few moments to review the menu while I get your drinks."

As we are reviewing the menu, the waitress reappears. "Here you go. Are you ready to order, or do you need a few more minutes?"

"We're ready," we say in unison.

"Ma'am, what can I get for you today?" she asks my mother.

"I'll have the shrimp alfredo and a side salad with ranch dressing."

She turns her attention to me and says, "And, you sir?"

"I'll have the lasagna and a side salad with ranch dressing.

"Got it. I will put your order in and be back shortly." She disappears.

"Jaxxson. I know how much hurt and pain you endured over the years. And, I know that you don't want to hear anything Jayyson has to say…but…I think it's time for you to hear him out."

"That's the same thing Charity and Pops told me."

"They're right. It's time to forgive. I know there has always been a part of you that still wants Jayyson in your life."

"Yeah," I admit.

"There's a lot of talk in the news. This may be one of the few chances that you have left to talk to him. It's not going to erase everything that went on when you were a child, but at least you can heal the last part of you that needs healing."

"What do you mean?" I ask.

"Sweetheart, at one point, you and Jayyson were super close. Your bond broke when he didn't believe you."

Gabriella reappears. "Here you go... shrimp alfredo for you, ma'am. And, lasagna for you, sir. Also, side salads with ranch dressing. What else can I get for you?"

"That's it," I respond.

"Alright. I will be back to check on you shortly."

"Thanks, Gabriella."

She nods in agreement as she goes to check on her other customers.

Mom continues, "I thank God every day for bringing Germaine into our lives. He has helped you to become the smart, strong, and independent young man that you are today. But, I know you...there is still some part of you that wishes Jayyson had been in your life throughout the years. And, I'm sure you missed having your big brothers in your life as well."

"Yeah, but I can't hold on to those dreams forever. I don't want my feelings towards Jada and Jayyson to continue holding me back. At some point, I would like to get married and have children. I haven't dated in years. I haven't even attempted to talk to women. I mean…I have talked to women as friends but not romantically," I admit.

"Exactly. It's time to heal."

We change our conversation and talk about anything but Jayyson as we enjoy our meals. As if she timed our last bite, Gabriella reappears.

"Do you need anything else?" she asks.

"Just the check, please," I reply.

"Yes, sir. Here you go."

I pay the bill and leave Gabriella a generous tip. Then, I escort Mama back to my car.

"Thanks, Mama!" I say as I start the ignition.

"For what?"

"For never giving up on me. I imagine there were many days that you were tempted. I know I was a handful growing up. No matter how hard things got, you never turned your back on me. I am truly grateful for everything you've done for me."

"You don't have to thank me, Jaxxson. Yes, we have been through a lot of trials and tribulations. There were days when I thought those storms would never cease. But, we overcame them with nothing but the grace of God. You are my son, and I would never give up on you. I will always have your back."

"I love you, Mama!"

"I love you, Jaxx!"

We embrace in a hug. I take Mama back to work and then I head home... Today turned out to be a pretty good day! Talking to Pops and Mama really helped. I feel so much better. Thank you, Lord! But, Mama brought up something that I never even considered... my brothers... I haven't seen or talked to them in years. It would have been nice to have my big brothers in my life. Let's see... Justin is twenty-nine years old, and Jerome is twenty-eight. When I left Jayyson's house that night, my relationship with my brothers ended. We didn't have a way to get in contact with them. Plus, my behavior prevented me from a lot of interaction with other people. For a while, Charity and Mama were the only ones that I could handle being around without any problems. Everybody else irritated me so bad that I would blow up. I'm glad that I finally got that under control.

Justin and Jerome. Justin was always the reasonable one. Jerome was a little all over the place. We were so close – my siblings and me. When Mama and Jayyson were married, she always made sure we spent time together as a family and included my brothers even though they weren't her biological children. I recall one of the times my dad was going to pick them up.

"Jayyson, what time are you picking up Justin and Jerome?" my mom asked.

"I'm about to leave now."

"Good. What are we doing while they're here?"

"Just hang out at the house."

"Not. They're kids. They do not want to be cooped up in the house. What about the fair? I think it's in town."

"Okay," he agreed.

Charity ran into the room. "Daddy, can we ride with you?"

"Of course, Charity. Come on, Jaxxson. Desirae, the kids are going with me."

"Alright. I'll be ready by the time you get back…"
The phone rings and interrupts my thoughts.

"Hello," I answer.

"Hey Jaxx? Are you okay?"

"Hey, Charity. I'm fine. Why?"

"I called you at work, but Mr. Jessup said that you were out sick."

"Oh yeah. I'm okay. I just needed a few days to get my mind right."

"Are you sure?" she pries.

"Yes, I'm okay. Actually, I went to see Pops and Mama today. I just got home not too long ago."

"I was getting worried."

"I love you, too. I'm fine. I was going to call you to see if you wanted to go to dinner later this week."

"That will be fine."

"I'll call you later this week. I love you, sis.

"I love you too, bro."

I decide to spend the next two days relaxing and catching up on my sleep, and then I get back to regularly scheduled programming. Thursday morning, I wake up completely refreshed and ready to return to work. I perform my usual morning routine and head into the office.

Chapter Four

"**G**ood morning, Jaxxson! Are you feeling better?"

"Good morning, Mr. Jessup. Yes, much better. Those few days of rest really did me a lot of good. Thank you for asking."

"Good. Are you ready to get back to work?"

"Yes sir."

"Well, all the projects are still on schedule. We have a meeting scheduled for next week to go over all the technicians' project updates. You will see the invite in your email."

"Yes sir. I will make sure to accept the invite. And, I will be ready for the meeting."

"I have no doubt in my mind about that, Jaxxson. You are one of my top performers. I'll let you get to work. It's good to have you back."

"Thank you, sir!"

Mr. Jessup leaves my office. I spend the next two days playing catch up on my workload. Friday arrives. I need to make sure that Charity can still make dinner tonight, so I give her a call. She answers on the first ring.

"What's up, Jaxx?"

"Are you still able to make dinner tonight?"

"Yes."

"Great! I will pick you up from your house at 7:00 p.m."

"Okay. I love you."

"I love you too."

I end the call and think about what I can do until dinnertime. I have so much energy, and I'm ready to get the workday finished. I spend the remainder of my day in my office. I'm so focused on completing my current projects that time has flown by quickly. I look at the clock on my wall and see that it's six o'clock already. I do one last check over all of my projects to make sure they're complete. Then, I grab my keys and lockup. As I'm headed out, I see Mr. Jessup in his office.

"Enjoy your weekend, Jaxxson," he says.

"I will. Are you headed out soon?" I ask as I stop to chat with him.

"Yes, I'm finishing this last thing and then I'm gone."

"Great! Have a good weekend," I say.

I leave the office and head to Charity's house. Traffic is the normal stop and go traffic. Everyone's in a rush to start their weekend. It amazes me that people are in such a rush to go nowhere. Patience is so scarce these days. *"Lord, keep us all safe as we travel to our various destinations,"* I pray silently. Finally, I arrive at Charity's house. She opens the door before I can even knock.

"Hey sis. Where do you want to go for dinner?"

"I'm not really hungry. We can just go up the street to Pearlie's Pynk Grille."

"Okay. Let's roll."

She locks up her house and then we head for my car. Naturally, I open the door and wait for my sister to get seated before I close the door. I get in and start the car.

"How was work?" she asks.

"It was pretty good. I got all my projects caught up. How are things going with you?"

"That's good. I had to let one of my supervisors go on Wednesday."

"Really?"

"Yeah. I hated to do it, but there was no other option. He had been coming to work drunk."

"Oh wow. Well, I'm sure you did what you had to do."

"Yeah. He had already been on disciplinary probation for job performance. He used to be one of my top supervisors."

"Really? What changed?" I quiz.

"I think he was having some family problems."

"Hopefully, he will be able to work through his problems. Here we go," I say as I find a parking spot.

I help Charity out the car as usual, and we walk inside. Pearlie's Pynk Grille is a small bistro-style restaurant. We have a seat at one of the tables on the patio. Strings of lights are strewn across the ceiling of the patio. The ceiling fans are generating a faint breeze throughout the area. There are various small white tables with matching chairs beside them. There's a young couple sitting on the opposite side of the patio.

A young man with freshly twisted dreads approaches our table and says, "My name is Douglas, and I will be your waiter this evening. What can I get you two to drink?

Charity says, "I will have a vanilla latte."

"And, I will have a sweet tea. Can I order the club sandwich with plain chips?" I add.

"Yes sir. What would you like to order, Miss?"

"Just the latte for me. Thanks."

"I will be right back with your drinks and your food, sir."

I thank Douglas as he's walking away. "Charity, are you okay?

"Why do you ask?"

"Because you are only getting a latte. That's not normal for you.

"I'm fine," she says plainly.

"Are you sure?"

"Yes, I'm sure."

"If you say so…" I say as I drop the subject.

Douglas reappears. "Here is your latte, miss. And your sweet tea, club sandwich, and plain chips, sir. Can I get you two anything else?"

"No, we're good."

Douglas leaves to tend to his other customers.

"Do you want half of my sandwich?" I offer to my sister.

"No, thank you. I'm good."

"What's wrong, sis? Something is obviously bothering you."

"It's just that… I have been a little worried about you. I know that you have been struggling with Jayyson's arrest, nightmares, and him calling you."

"Yeah. It has been a rollercoaster of emotions these last few months."

"Are you mad at me, Jaxx?"

"Why would I be mad at you?"

"Because I knew Jayyson was going to call you, and I didn't give you a heads up."

"No, I'm not upset with you. I was upset with the whole situation with Jayyson not believing me and being absent from our lives. Talking to Pops and Mama helped a lot. I realized that there are still some parts of me that need healing," I admit.

"Like what?"

"There is a part of me that wishes Jayyson had been in my life over the years."

"Understandable, Jaxx."

"And, I would like to get married and have children one day. But, in order for that to happen, I have to find a wife. I haven't dated in years. I want to make sure I deal with my issues before getting romantically involved with someone."

"I think that is a wise thing to do," Charity replies.

Douglas reappears and asks, "Can I get you anything else?"

"Just the check, please."

"Here you go, sir."

I pay the bill and leave Douglas a generous tip.

Douglas responds, "Thank you. Have a good evening," as he's leaving.

"You as well, Douglas." I wait for him to disappear and then I continue, "There are parts of me that wish I still had a relationship with Justin and Jerome as well."

"Justin and Jerome... Wow, we haven't heard from them in years! I always assumed Jayyson kept them away from us."

"We won't know for certain until we talk to him."

There is a glimmer of excitement in her voice. "Does this mean that you will go with me to see him in a couple of weeks?" my sister asks.

"Yes. I still have a lot of unanswered questions. Unfortunately, he is the only one that can answer them."

"Jaxxson, I am proud of you. You have grown a lot! You had to deal with a lot as a child. I am so glad that you were able to overcome it."

"I'm still not completely over it."

"Yeah...but...you have come a long way!" Charity says.

"That's true. And, Mama brought up something that I haven't considered."

"What?"

"I want to get back in contact with our brothers. Let's get their contact information when we go see Jayyson."

"I agree! I miss my brothers."

Chapter Five

"Jerome, are you ready?"

"I'm as ready as I'm gonna get, Justin!"

Justin and Jerome walk into the sanctuary just in time for the morning message. They have a seat on one of the back pews. Pastor Grace is already at the podium.

"It seems like every time I turn on the TV or listen to the radio, there's a story about children being abused. They are being abused physically... emotionally... and sexually! It breaks my heart to hear that they're enduring such pain from the very person put in place to protect them. Yes, it happens with strangers as well. But, it's primarily someone in the family or close to the family. What kind of person could bring any harm to an innocent child? What kind of person can fix their minds to view a two-year-old... six-year-old... nine-year-old child as a sexual being? Lord, help us!

"As I'm praying for these babies, I'm asking God for clarity. Why would a grown man or woman inflict such pain on these babies? Children don't have the mental capacity to even understand what is being done to them. Let alone how to handle it when it happens. Sometimes the abuse continues for weeks, months, or years. What's wrong with the world? You know what God revealed when I asked Him?"

The congregation responds, "What?

"God revealed that the sad truth is that it was done to them These abusers were once innocent little boys and girls. Unfortunately, they never told what Cousin Bobby… or Uncle Henry… or Aunt Susie Q was doing to them. Their abuser probably used some scare tactic to keep the child from telling… No one will believe you… This is your fault… You made me do this… If you tell, I will kill your family! Sometimes, they tell the children that it's a game. It's our special secret and you can't tell anyone! All of these are just different forms of manipulation to gain control and keep the children silent.

"These abusers are relying on the children remaining silent so that they can continue to get away with it. Unfortunately, some of the children never told or got the help needed to heal. So, they turned around and abused someone else. They became a predator! This is not saying that everyone who is abused as a child will become a predator as an adult. But, it's a possibility. It's a sad reality! This is not a topic that is discussed enough in the homes. That's the problem. Not enough discussion about important topics… Abuse is a very important topic."

The congregation listens and "Amen" rings throughout the congregation as Pastor Grace continues.

"Parents, talk to your children about the difference between a good touch and a bad touch. Stop being so quick to let them go over to the next-door neighbor's house to play or spend the night! Same for going over relatives' houses... I know you are expecting your children to be safe because you know them. And, they may be safe, but you don't know what's happening in everybody's household! Abuse has been happening to children for many generations. It's coming out more now because children are speaking up for themselves. Sadly, it's an unfortunate cycle. It's part of a generational curse that has plagued families for centuries... What happens in the family, stays in the family... Don't listen to that load of crap!

"Anytime someone or something is causing you harm, tell it! Tell a parent, aunt, uncle, teacher, school counselor, etc. If you tell someone and they don't listen, continue telling until someone hears you. Tell anyone who will listen! I guarantee you that someone will listen and help! It's time to use your voice and speak up for yourself! Don't allow your voices to be silenced anymore!

First Lady Laiyah chimes in, "Amen! Speak up!"

The congregation responds, "Amen" while clapping their hands.

"Unfortunately, we always hear about children being abused, but we never hear about the after effect it has on the child. Some children are constantly being triggered into reliving the trauma on a daily basis. Pay attention to your children! Every child reacts differently. If your child or children suddenly start acting out… not speaking… becomes withdrawn… suddenly wears extra baggy clothes… hesitates when that family friend comes around… becomes violent… begins stealing… skips school... You need to do some investigating! These are not automatic guarantees that they are being abused, but something is going on with them.

"It is very important to create an open dialogue with them. Talk to them. And LISTEN to what they say. Children who don't heal from abuse as a child, grow up to be adults with some serious problems. Sadly, they don't always survive to become adults. Some have just accepted it and are functioning. They put on a front like everything is okay. Take the time to think about the psychological effects that it has on them. Typically, children struggle to express their feelings. Just imagine suffering from abuse on top of normal childhood struggles. It's horrible! I imagine that could destroy a person's mental health.

"Today's society is a lot different from how it was twenty or thirty plus years ago. Back in the day, children were meant to be seen not heard. They always had to do whatever their elders told them. They definitely couldn't participate in conversations with adults. Today, they are still supposed to listen to their elders, but it's okay to say no to something that is wrong! Children have a voice and are encouraged to use it!"

"Amen," and clapping hands sound all around the sanctuary.

"Thank you, Holy Spirit. The altar workers are coming. Originally, I planned to speak on a different topic. About fifteen minutes before I stepped to this podium, I was given a new message. God said for me to speak on this topic. So, I did as I was told I know this message is specific to someone. If you have a personal struggle with abuse, God says, it's over! Your healing has already begun! Come to the altar, and we will pray for your strength. If this is not your personal struggle but you know someone who has dealt with abuse, come to the altar. God says it's okay to seek professional help."

Again, the congregation agrees. Pastor Grace continues, "Society has us believing that we are not supposed to go to therapy. If you go to therapy, you're crazy. Don't discuss our family business with a stranger. Just go to church and pray about it. Prayer and church are always good, but sometimes it's better to speak with a neutral party about your issues. There are trained professionals that will help you. They will guide you through the journey of healing. Don't be ashamed to ask for help! You have been silent long enough! Use your voice!"

The altar becomes flooded with young and old who need prayer. "Amen" continues to ring throughout the sanctuary.

Jerome looks at Justin with tears in his eyes. Justin asks, "Do you want to go for prayer?" Jerome looks at him but is unable to speak.

Justin's eyes begin to fill with tears and says, "I'll walk with you." His brother nods in agreement. They join hands and walk down the aisle to the altar. The congregation erupts in "Amen" and clapping hands. Deacon Ashby joins hands with them as he begins to pray for them.

Charity whispers, "Jaxxson, are you okay?"

With tears in my eyes, I whisper, "Yes, I'm okay. The message just hit a little too close to home; that's all."

"Do you want to go for prayer?"

"No, I'll be okay."

"Are you sure? I will walk with you," she says.

"Thanks, sis. I'm okay."

Again, the congregation erupts in "Amen" as more people head to the altar for prayer.

Again, Charity whispers, "Jaxxson. Look at the two guys at the altar with Deacon Ashby… Don't they look like Jayyson?"

I stare at the guys for a moment. *Justin and Jerome?* Charity and I realize our brothers are standing at the altar. We immediately join them. They turn around after receiving prayer. Charity and I are standing behind them with tears in our eyes. We all embrace, and the tears begin to flow like rivers.

The congregation is clapping and singing, "Hallelujah! Praise God!" Pastor Grace has tears streaming down his face as he realizes the whole congregation has come and gone from prayer.

"Father, thank you! Thank you! Thank you! There is healing happening all around us today. Thank you, Lord! We needed this message!"

First Lady Laiyah has tears flowing while shouting, "Hallelujah! Thank you, Father! Thank you!"

Mother Hensley says, "Praise God!"

The congregation sings, "Amen, Amen. Thank you, Lord!"

Pastor Grace says, "Everyone has a storm that they must go through. Sometimes you have to just dance in the rain! Someone is at their breaking point of giving up! Someone is contemplating suicide right now! Don't let the storm destroy you! Don't give up! Come to the altar for prayer!"

A young lady walks to the altar with tears flowing like a river. Sister Celine, Deaconess Ashby, and First Lady join her for support.

"Amen! Thank you, Father! Continue to pray and ask God for His guidance. Trust what He tells you! Trust what He shows you! We all struggle with our inner demons. Your demon may not be abuse. It may be depression, drug addiction, alcohol addiction, promiscuity, or domestic violence. I want everyone to come to the altar and join hands."

Everyone walks to the altar and joins hands as instructed.

"Dear Heavenly Father, thank you! Thank you for today's message. Thank you for the healing that is taking place! So many have been hurt by abuse. So many have struggled with moving forward. They have been broken by generational curses. Lord, we are ready! Please continue to place Your angels of protection around them as they go through this journey. We know that this road will not be easy, but we are ready! We are here to help those in need… anyway that we can. Grant them with the discernment to know who is for them and who is against them! Renew their faith! Renew their trust! These and other blessings, I pray. Amen. You are all dismissed." The crowd disperses.

Charity greets our brothers with hugs. "It's so good to see you, Justin and Jerome. We have missed you both. Jaxx and I were just talking about getting back in contact with you guys."

"Jerome and I have missed you as well. Can we go somewhere and talk?"

Charity responds, "Of course."

Pops and Mama appear from the dispersed crowd.

"These are our brothers, Justin and Jerome."

Pops extends a hand for both and says, "Nice to meet you guys."

Justin responds, "Nice to meet you, sir," while shaking hands.

Then, Jerome responds, "Nice to meet you" and also shakes Pops' hand.

Mama greets them as well. They both wave hello.

"We won't be at Sunday dinner, today. We're going somewhere to talk to our brothers. Pops, can you take my car over your house? I'm going to ride with Jaxxson," Charity adds.

"Of course, sweetheart."

"Thank you. We will come by later."

"You're welcome," Pops says as he and Mama walk away.

"What about the Red Bottom Restaurant downtown?" I ask.

"'That will be fine."

"Okay. We'll see you guys there in about fifteen minutes."

Justin and Jerome get in their car and head that way. Charity and I get in my car and do the same.

Chapter Six

We all pull up at the restaurant at same time and enter together.
The hostess asks, "How many?"
Charity replies, "Four."
"Right this way."
We follow the hostess. "Here we go," she says while placing our menus on the table. "Your waitress will be with you shortly.
We take our seats and begin looking at our menus.
The waitress appears. "My name is Alyssa, and I will be your waitress. What can I get you to drink?"
Charity says, "I'll have water with lemon."
Justin, Jerome, and I request water with no lemon.
"Okay. I'll give you a few moments to review the menu while I get your drinks."
As we are reviewing the menus, Alyssa reappears.
"Here you go. Are you ready to order, or do you need a few more minutes?"
"We're ready."
Charity says, "I'll have the grilled chicken salad with ranch dressing."

Justin says, "I'll have the steak - medium well - with loaded mashed potatoes and broccoli."

Jerome says, "I'll have the same but a well-done steak."

"I'll have the blackened salmon and rice pilaf," Justin adds.

"Got it. I will put your order in and be back shortly."

"Thank you, Alyssa." As she walks away, I spark up a conversation. "It's been a long, long time. It's good to see you guys. So, what made you two decide to come to church today?"

"Actually, Jerome and I were looking for you and Charity. We didn't have any contact information for you but remembered you attended that church."

"So, what's on your mind?" I ask.

Justin and Jerome look at each other and take deep breaths. Justin says, "I'm so sorry about what Jada did to you. I didn't know."

"Yeah, but it's not your fault." Charity rubs my shoulder for sympathy.

Jerome says, "I'm so sorry that I didn't say anything sooner."

Charity and I look at each other with confusion on our faces.

"What do you mean, Jerome?" she asks.

Shame covers his face, and his eyes begin to fill with tears. Justin rubs his shoulder for empathy. Jerome looks down and says, "Jada started with me when I was nine years old, too."

Sadness covers our faces. "Bro, I'm so sorry! It's not your fault!"

Alyssa reappears and places the food on the table accordingly. "Do you need anything else?

"No, we're good," we say in unison.

"Okay. I'll check back on you shortly." Alyssa disappears.

Jerome says, "Jaxxson, I'm proud of you for speaking up when it happened."

"I am proud of you, Jerome."

"Thanks, sis. I'm a work in progress. I'm taking it one day at a time."

"Amen," we say.

"What's been going on with you, Justin?" I ask.

"My wife, Simone, and I welcomed a beautiful baby girl named Serenity Simone Craig a few months ago. Here, I have a picture." He reaches into his wallet and pulls out a picture of his family.

"They are beautiful! We can't wait to meet them both."

"Thanks, Jaxx! What have you two been doing?"

"I'm an Operations Manager and Jaxx is an Engineer Technician. All we do is work," Charity laughs.

"Nothing wrong with that!"

"I'm sorry that it took us years to reconnect," she adds.

Jerome says, "Daddy told us that Desirae was keeping you two from coming around us."

"That's not true. Jayyson never attempted to contact Mama. After the night I told him, that was it. I hadn't heard a word from him. When was the last time you've talked to or seen him?" I ask.

Justin and Jerome look at each other. Jerome says, "Not since the night I finally told him about what Jada did to me. I told him a couple days before he killed Jada."

"That's it! I was wondering what finally sent him over the edge to kill her."

Jerome responds with disappointment in his voice, "It was me."

"You are not to blame for this mess! Jada was the one who took advantage of you... me... and Lord knows who else!"

"You're right," he says.

"Jerome, we're here for you! Anytime you need us, we will be there!"

"Thanks Charity."

Justin chimes in, "I almost forgot. We talked to Greydon. He told us that daddy wrote each of us a letter before killing Jada. Daddy made him promise to give us the letters. We told him that we were getting back in contact with you guys. He gave us your letters. Here you go." He hands Charity and me the letters. "We have ours, too." They hold up their letters. "We wanted to wait to read them with you."

We stare at the envelopes.

Justin asks, "Who wants to go first?"

Charity breaks the silence and says, "I will."

"Are you sure?"

"Yes. I'm sure, Justin." She begins to read:

Dear Charity,

My sweet little princess. I have missed you so much! I am so sorry that I destroyed our family. I know that I should have been a better father! I should have been a better man! I want you know that I never stopped loving you. I think about you every day. I still carry that picture of you and me at your 3rd grade Daddy/Daughter dance in my wallet every day. That was always one of the happiest days of my life.

I know that you have heard some unpleasant things about me in the news lately. Though it is true that I killed Jada, I don't want that to be your last memory of me. I have missed so much of your life. I don't want to miss anymore. I hope that you will allow me back into your life someday. I love you! And, I will be reaching out to you soon!

Love,
Daddy

She has tears in her eyes, but she's smiling. "The third grade dance! He still carried that picture. I thought he forgot about me. But, he didn't!" She wipes away the tears. "Justin, why don't you go next?

"Ok." He begins to read:

Dear Justin,

You were right! I fucked up royally! It was my responsibility to protect my kids. And, I failed your brothers! I never could have imagined anything like this happening. Sadly, I have to accept the fact that my wife is a pedophile…and she abused two of my boys! I made a huge mistake bringing Jada into our lives. That is a mistake that I must live with for the rest of my life. Unfortunately, I cannot undo the harm that she has caused our family. I want you to know that I am very proud of you! You have turned out to be a better man that I could ever hope. I know that you will be an excellent father. You were right to take Jerome and leave. I know you will make sure he gets the help that he needs from here on out.

By now, I'm sure you know that I killed Jada. And, I'm sure you know why I did it. I'm ashamed that I allowed myself to be manipulated by her all these years. But, I couldn't allow her to hurt anyone else. I hope that one day you can find it in your heart to forgive me. I love you!

Love,
Daddy

Justin has tears in his eyes. "He's proud of me. I'm glad that he finally recognized that he messed up our family. Jerome, are you ready?"

"I guess so." Jerome begins to read:

Dear Jerome,
I am proud of you for speaking your truth! I imagine that could not have been an easy thing for you to do. I honestly never imagined that my wife would abuse my children. I am sorry that I didn't do a better job of

56

protecting you. If I could turn back the hands of time, Jada never would have entered the picture. I wish I could undo all the pain you suffered over the years. I know that my words can never erase the pain and anger that you feel. You were right to leave with Justin. I trust that he will do everything within his power to help you through the process of healing.

I wish I could be there to help you, but I'm sure word has gotten out that I killed Jada. I just couldn't let her continue to get away with what she did to you and Jaxxson. I'm sorry that I have been blind for so many years. I never meant to put you in harm's way! I really hope that one day you can find it in your heart to forgive me. I love you.

Love,
Daddy

"Well, I guess it's my turn," I say as tears fill Jerome's eyes. I begin to read:

Dear Jaxxson,
I have missed you! I think about all the times we would make our morning run for donuts. Just you and me. You would ride shotgun, and I would crank up the volume on whatever was playing. I can't help but smile at the memories. I know you're angry at me for turning my back on you, Charity, and Desirae. I am truly sorry that I didn't believe you. You had never lied to me about anything in the past. And, I should have trusted that you weren't lying to me at that moment. I definitely should have asked more

questions instead of just brushing it off without another thought. That thought is on repeat in my head daily. Why didn't I pay attention to the signs?

I wish that I could go back to that moment in time. I promise I would handle that situation a lot better. Unfortunately, I can never undo the past! I'm sure that you heard the news of me killing Jada. I had to make sure she was stopped. I know it will take some time, but I hope you can find it in your heart to forgive me. I will be in contact soon. I love you!

Love,
Daddy

Everyone has tears in their eyes. "Why couldn't he have said all this years ago?" I ask.

Charity responds, "I don't know Jaxx. We have to focus on moving forward and rebuilding our relationship with our brothers. Let's just focus on the positive."

Alyssa reappears and asks, "How are you guys doing?"

"We're good. Can we have the check?" I ask.

"Sure. Will this be on separate tickets or one?"

"One."

"No. Jaxx, you don't have to do that," Justin says.

"It's fine. Someone else can pay next time. Just one ticket, Alyssa."

"Yes sir. Here you go."

I pay the bill. As usual, I leave Alyssa a generous tip before she leaves us. "Thanks for bringing the letters. I'm glad you guys came to church. We have to stay in contact from here on out." We exchange contact information. "Justin and Jerome, do you want to hangout next weekend?

They respond in unison, "Yes."

"Great! I'll reach out to you guys next week, and we can discuss the details."

Justin says, "Sounds like a plan to me."

"Me too," Jerome adds.

We all embrace and head our separate ways.

"Jaxxson, can you take me to my car?"

"Of course," I reply to my sister. Then, we head to Mama and Pops. "That was a pretty good visit. It was so good to see them after all these years."

"Yeah. I'm so glad that we're going to stay in touch. What do you think about Jayyson writing us letters?" she asks.

"I was completely surprised."

"Me too. I didn't expect that at all," I reply.

Charity has a puzzled look on her face.

"What's wrong, Charity?"

"It's just that… I thought he didn't think about us over the years. But, he did! He thought about us all the time."

"It appears that way."

"Well…If that's the case, why didn't he take the time to be in our lives?"

"I don't know. Maybe that's something to ask when we go see him."

"Yeah. I guess I have some unanswered questions as well," she says.

"Understandable."

We arrive at our parents' home and walk in. Charity shouts, "Mama? Pops?"

Pops responds, "We're in the den."

We join them, and Mama asks, "How did everything go?"

"Everything went good, Mama. We're going to stay in contact and work on rebuilding our relationship."

"That's great, Jaxxson!"

"Mama, can I ask you something?" Charity says.

"What's on your mind?"

"Did Jayyson ever reach out over the years?"

"Why do you ask?"

"Jayyson told Justin and Jerome that you were keeping us from coming around."

"Of course, he did. Jayyson had a bad habit of pushing the blame on everybody but himself. I reached out to him several times for help after Jaxxson kept getting suspended from school and lost his memory. All he did was push the blame on me. Everything was always my fault in his eyes. I got fed up with him blaming me for everything. So, I stopped reaching out to him."

"Mama, he blamed you for my problems?"

"Yes, Jaxxson."

"But, you were not to blame for any of my problems. All you did was help me! Jayyson is part of the blame!"

"Thank you, sweetheart! Jayyson did call me once…." Mom recalls the conversation.

"Hi, Desirae."

"Hi, Jayyson."

"Where are the kids?"

"Well, since it is 11:00 p.m., they're asleep," she replied.

"Oh, yeah… How are you doing?"

"I'm good."

"That's good. Can you tell them that I'm sorry, and I love them?" Jayyson said.

"What's wrong?"

"I'm just tired of life. Every time I try to do the right thing, it turns out bad. This is not how I wanted us to be. We were supposed to be together forever."

"What happened?" mama asked.

"I just been thinking about a lot of stuff. You and I were always able to talk. We used to talk for hours about any and everything under the sun. Do you remember?"

"Yes, I remember. But, we are not on that level anymore. Remember, you chose Jada over me when you cheated on me. You should be able to talk to her about anything now."

"I can't talk to her like I can talk to you. There's a lot of stuff that she doesn't understand. She doesn't know

me the way you do. I miss you so much. And, I love you," he said.

Silence…

"Desirae!"

More silence…

"Desirae, did you hear me?" he said.

Finally, she replied, "I heard you, Jayyson."

"You don't miss me? You don't love me?"

"At one point, I loved you more than life itself. I miss the Jayyson that I fell in love with years ago. Unfortunately, that's not who you are anymore. You turned your back on your family for a woman that you barely know. I can't love a man that would do that. You should be talking to your wife, not me!"

"Please tell my babies that I love them. I can't take this life anymore," he said and ended the call.

"He hung up on me," she says.

"He was threatening suicide and you didn't help him?"

"It's not that I didn't want to help him, Charity. He has said all that before in the past."

"What do you mean?" she asks.

"Jayyson has threatened to commit suicide multiple times over the years. And, each time, he called me. I would drop everything I was doing just to help him. For a brief moment, he was back to being dedicated to his family. Eventually, he went back to doing the same things that had him suicidal in the first place. I asked him several times to go to therapy, and he refused to go. Greydon tried to get him to go, but he refused! My priorities were you and Jaxxson. Since Jayyson didn't want to help himself, I couldn't help him. I didn't have time to waste on his empty promises anymore. And, I knew that he wouldn't hurt himself."

Charity asks, "How did you know?"

"Because he would have done it already."

"Did you know about this, Pops?" I ask.

"Yes, Jaxxson. Desirae and I talk about everything. We don't have secrets from each other."

I turn to my mom for answers. "Why didn't you tell us, Mama?"

"It was just a form of manipulation to get close to me. He knew that I loved him and wanted him to be safe. Normally, I would put my plans on hold to get him back on track. Every time I helped him, it took forever for me to get my plans back on track. I didn't want to go through that endless cycle anymore. I wanted better for you, Charity, and myself. There's a side of Jayyson that I've tried to keep away from you and Charity."

I ask, "What side?"

"That's not important, Jaxxson. I don't want to add to your bad feelings towards Jayyson. That side is between me and Jayyson. Germaine knows about it. Just focus on bonding with your brothers. You guys have a lot of catching up to do."

"You're right!"

"Don't let this cause any additional ill feelings towards Jayyson. He has his faults, but no one is perfect!"

"We won't, Mama..." Charity and I agree.

"When are y'all getting together with Justin and Jerome again?"

"I'm going to hang out with them on Saturday."

Charity chimes in, "Yeah. I figured they needed some brother bonding time. But, we're all getting together Sunday after church."

"They're coming to church again?"

"Yeah, Pops. Justin is bringing his wife and baby girl."

"That's great! Why don't y'all just come over for Sunday dinner?"

"I will check with them. Oh, and I was thinking of bringing Justin and Jerome over to the program on Saturday."

"I think that's a great idea!"

"Great! It's been a long day. I think I'm going to head home."

"Me too," I say.

"We love you both," Mama says.

My sister and I reply, "We love you, too."

Chapter Seven

I hear a knock on my door. I open it without looking through the peephole because I already know it's my brothers.

"Hey, I'm glad you guys made it. Come on in and make yourself at home."

They walk in and admire my three-bedroom, two-bathroom home. In my living room, I have a smoky gray oversized sectional with matching chair, glass top coffee and end tables with black wrought iron base, two black floor vases with birch branch red, a 65'' flat screen TV mounted on the wall, and some red, black, and gray picture frames with family pictures in them.

"You have a beautiful home, Jaxx."

"Thanks, Jerome."

Justin says, "And, I love the artwork on your wall. Who is the artist?"

"Thanks, man!" I say while laughing. "I'm the artist!"

Jerome asks, "Really?"

I nod in agreement.

"These are great!" He takes a closer look. "Wait… is that you?"

"Yes. That's one of my favorite pictures. I call it 'Showers of Inspiration.'" I describe the image. "Rain clouds fill the sky. Inspirational words like *faith, blessings, grace, mercy, favor, peace, love, live, happiness, joy,* and *hope* are falling from the clouds like rain showers. I'm standing on the ground with my arms open wide ready to receive inspiration."

"That's amazing, Jaxx!"

"Thanks bro."

Justin asks, "What about this one?"

"That's another favorite picture. I call it 'Breeze of Peace.' Clear blue water illuminates the sandy white beach. Beautiful blue skies with sun rays are peaking from behind the clouds. My best friend, Earnest, is lounging in the hammock next to the palm trees. He passed away a few years ago. This picture depicts how I want to remember him… at peace."

They respond, "I'm sorry, Jaxx. That's a nice way to remember him."

"Yeah. It helps me keep my sanity."

Justin asks, "Are these pictures the only artwork you've created?"

I laugh because my collection goes far beyond what they see. "No," I reply as I guide them to one of the bedrooms. "This is my room of art."

I flip the light switch.

"This room is filled with all the art that I've created since childhood. It has the good… the bad… and the ugly."

They admire my artwork for a few moments. Then, we return to the living room.

"Man, those are great! You have a talent for art!" Jerome says proudly.

"Thanks! It's just a hobby of mine."

Justin adds, "It's something that you should definitely let the world see."

"Nah, it's just something I do for me."

"Yeah, but you tell a story through your art. That's important!"

"Maybe I will… one day. Can I get you guys something to drink?"

"Water is fine," they agree.

I get some water bottles from the fridge and hand one to each of them. Then, we have a seat on the couch.

"I was thinking that I would take you guys by the Building Better Men Program. This program and Pops helped me so much when I was growing up."

"Sounds good to me," Justin says.

"First, can I ask you something?" Jerome asks.

"Sure."

"After the abuse from Jada, did you get into a lot of fights in school?"

"Man, all the time! I got into so much trouble that I kept causing Mama to lose her jobs. So, she started sitting in my classroom to make sure that I didn't get into any trouble. It worked if she was right there. I remember one time when I was nine years old… Mama was in my classroom, but she had an errand to run. When my class went outside for recess, she figured that would be a good time to leave. I wanted to go with her, but she wouldn't let me. She told me to play with my friends until she came back in thirty minutes. I decided to play basketball with my friend, Sylvester.

"Now, Braylen was a known bully. He decided to start making comments about Mama. He called Mama fat and ugly. He just wanted to get me in trouble because he knew that I would react. Naturally, I reacted. I walked over to him and asked him to repeat what he said about Mama. As he repeats it, my fists are already balled up. I'm ready to fight! Mr. Alexander, the teacher's aide, saw me and quickly ran between us. He caught my fist in mid-swing. Braylen was standing behind Mr. Alexander laughing at me. Mr. Alexander asked what happened. I told him that Braylen was talking about my Mama. Of course, Braylen denied it! Mr. Alexander told Braylen to walk away and go play. Then, he stayed and talked to me for a few minutes. I have no idea what he said because I stopped listening.

"At that moment, I was in revenge mode. I knew that I was going to get Braylen back for talking about Mama. Mr. Alexander decided to take me to Principal Baxter's office to keep me from getting into trouble. I was supposed to stay there until Mama came back. At first, I was upset that I had to go to the office while Braylen got to continue playing. Then, I noticed all the security cameras in the office. And, guess who I see coming in from recess headed to the restroom?"

Jerome says, "Braylen?"

"Yep. So, I asked Mrs. Baxter if I could go to the restroom. She watched me and waited for a moment. Then, she asked me if I was calm. I told her I was. She believed me and let me to the restroom, but I had to hurry back. I left out of the office with a huge smile on my face. I went straight there and found Braylen. I finished what he started on the playground. I beat him so bad that he was left crying in the fetal position on the ground. It took Mr. Alexander and two security guards to pull me off him. They took me back to Mrs. Baxter's office and explained what I did. Mrs. Baxter called Mama, but she was already pulling into the parking lot.

"Mama walked in asking what happened. Principal Baxter told her I attacked a little boy in the restroom. She asked if the little boy was okay. The principal told her he was fine but just bruised up and his mom was on the way to the school. My Mama turned to me asked me why I beat Braylen up. I told her it was because he had been talking about her. She replied, 'Jaxxson, how many times have we had this conversation? I appreciate you wanting to protect me, but that's not an excuse to hurt someone. Don't worry about what people say about me. They are just looking to get you in trouble.'"

My brothers listen intently as I continue.

"Then, Mrs. Baxter asked me how I knew Braylen was in the restroom. I pointed to the cameras. She was impressed that I was smart enough to use the cameras to my advantage. But, she was disappointed that I hurt a student. Of course, I got suspended for three days, but I didn't care. I was happy because I didn't want to be there anyway. Braylen and the other kids learned not to talk about my Mama. I got suspended from school a lot." I said.

Justin adds, "I got into a lot of fights in school, too. I got suspended and expelled a couple of times as well. Jada messed up both our childhoods."

"Yes, she did!" I agree. "There was one time when I had a bad reaction to some medication. I believe I was ten years old. I hadn't slept at all that previous night. Suddenly, I started hallucinating. I was completely out of it. I kept trying to fight whatever images I was seeing in front of me. Mama rushed me to the emergency room at Children's Hospital. The doctors ended up giving me medicine to help me sleep and counteract the hallucinations. Eventually, I dozed off. I slept for a few hours. When I woke up, I was back to normal."

Jerome looks like he's in disbelief. "Wow! That had to be scary."

"Yes! The worst thing that resulted from the abuse was when I lost my memory," I say.

"You lost your memory?"

"Yes. It was shortly after the reaction to the medicine."

"How?"

"One night, Mama was in her bedroom watching TV. I was in Charity's bedroom, and we were talking as usual. Suddenly, I started crying and saying, 'Stop it! It hurts! It hurts!' Charity started yelling for Mama that something was wrong with me. She ran into the room asking what happened. She told her everything that happened. Then, Mama started shaking me and calling my name and telling me it was her.

"I stopped crying and was back normal. But, a few minutes later, I went into a childlike state, mentally and physically. I was literally talking and acting like a little kid. I didn't know who Mama, Charity, or anybody was at that point. Originally, I thought my mama, my aunt, and Charity were all my cousins. Auntie asked where my mama was. I told her that she was dead, and daddy was in jail because he killed her.

"Of course, Mama was trying not to freak out. She took me back to the emergency room at Children's Hospital. At that time, I had been taking medicine to help balance my moods. Initially, the doctors thought that I was having another reaction to the medicine. So, they stopped it. They said if it was the medicine, my memory would come back in a couple of days…"

"Did your memory come back in a couple of days?" Justin asks.

"Nope. I ended up going to a neurologist for an MRI to see if there was brain damage or something like that causing the memory loss. Mama had already explained to the neurologist what happened prior to me losing my memory and the constant nightmares from the abuse. She confirmed there was no brain damage and that I had a flashback to the trauma.

"Basically, something triggered the past trauma. She couldn't confirm what triggered it, but I kept reliving the trauma until it became too much for me to handle. My brain protected itself and blocked out everything. Mama had to reteach me everything – my name, how to eat, how to take care of my hygiene, my academics, and everything else. She had to reintroduce me to family members because I had no memory of them. Before I lost my memory, there were moments when I took my anger out on Charity. She would unintentionally say or do something to trigger the past trauma. It's like I would black out and go into attack mode. I would attack Charity, but I saw Jada in those moments. There was so much anger built up from the abuse and torture at the hands of Jada. Eventually, my memory came back. There was a lot of prayer, therapy, and help from Pops to get me back on track."

Justin says, "I am so sorry that you had to go through all that! That is a lot!"

Jerome says, "Yeah, I never lost my memory. I am so sorry that happened to you!"

"It wasn't an easy journey but I'm doing good. What about you, Jerome? I know that you had it worse than I did. You lived with her for years. I can't even imagine."

"Jada used to give me weed and alcohol on a regular basis. I became so addicted that I couldn't function without it. I used to sneak a sports bottle full of Hennessey and soda to school. I would sip on it throughout the day. I became a functioning alcoholic before I entered high school. There were days when I skipped school with some friends just to get high. When I did go to school, I would get into fight after fight. The slightest thing would set me off.

"There were many moments growing up that I wished that I was dead. I even attempted suicide once when I was eleven years old. I was fed up with the abuse. I took a bunch of pills because I was ready to end it all. But, it only gave me a really bad headache. There were so many times when I wanted to tell daddy, but I knew he wouldn't believe me. I told Jada multiple times that I couldn't do it anymore. I wanted it to stop! I even threatened to tell daddy, but she said he would blame me for it. All those years of mind games took me to the lowest points within my life. When I finally moved out, I vowed it would never happen again. There were times when I wanted to talk to you and Justin about what was happening. I just felt so embarrassed. I wasn't sure that you would believe me either."

"I would have believed you, Jerome. I would've made sure that shit never happened again! Even if daddy didn't believe it, I would have taken you down to the police station myself. I am sure that you and Jaxxson were not the only ones to be abused by Jada. There is no way that she suddenly woke up one day and decided to rape little boys."

Jerome asks, "Why? Why would she do that?"

"I do think that Pastor Grace was right in his sermon," I say.

"What do you mean?"

"Most likely, she was abused as a child and didn't get the help that she needed to heal."

"Maybe… but, that still doesn't give her the right to abuse someone else. If she was abused, she knew how it felt. Why inflict that pain on someone else?"

"You're right. But, I don't think we will ever know the answer to that question. How are you doing, Jerome?"

"Now, I'm good. I think the turning point was me finally telling my truth. I'm going to my therapy sessions weekly. I had been getting into a lot of trouble over the years. My lawyer was able to work out a plea deal for my DUI. I won't have to do any jail time if I stay out of trouble. I'm required to attend AA meetings, and meetings in the marijuana addiction program. Justin kept his promise by being with me through this whole process. And, I finally have you and Charity back in my life. Life is good. Once I told, it's like everything just started falling into place. The night leaving daddy's house made all the difference. He recalls that night.

"*Man, this has been one hell of a night! Jerome, stay away from daddy and Jada!*" Justin said.

"*I will! I have been carrying that weight around for nineteen years!*"

"*Why didn't you tell me or anybody?*"

"*Jada told me that no one would believe me. When daddy didn't believe Jaxxson, I figured she was right. So, I kept the secret!*"

"*Bro, I would have believed you! I would have made sure that you weren't living with her anymore! What about after you moved out on your own? Why not say something at that time?*"

Jerome says, "*I don't know. I guess I was still that fragile little boy that she manipulated for all those years. It's hard to get past all of it!*"

"*I'm so sorry!*"

"*It's not your fault, Justin! You didn't do anything wrong.*"

"*I'm sorry that you had to go through this for years. I really wish you had told me, but I understand why you didn't!*"

There's silence for a few minutes.

"*Jerome.*"

"*Yeah.*"

"*I think it would help if you talked to someone… a professional.*"

"You want me to talk to some shrink? I'm not crazy!"

"Bruh, I know you're not crazy. Like you said, you have had that weight on you for nineteen years. That's a long time to endure sexual abuse. Not to mention the psychological and emotional abuse. You will need someone who is specifically trained to help you through all of it."

"No. I'm good."

"Jerome! You are not good. Think about it...the weed...alcohol...fights over the years since childhood. All that so you can cover up the pain and hurt that you suffered for years! Maybe your attorney can get your sentence reduced or something?" Justin said.

"No. I don't want anyone to know that I was raped by my stepmother. That shit is so embarrassing!"

"Bruh, that's the problem! I understand you don't want anyone to know. You kept the secret for so long that it just about destroyed you. It's time to let it out so that you can heal from it! It won't be an easy process, but it will be well worth the journey. This is the next step to getting your life back on track. Bruh, you need a fresh start. You deserve it. And I will be there every step of the way," Justin said.

"You promise?"

"Yes, I promise. I will not abandon you!"

Jerome finally agreed, "Okay. I will try it."

"I'll call your attorney in the morning to setup a time for us to come in and talk. Once we get you back in a positive direction, we will reach out to Charity and Jaxxson. We really need to repair that relationship."

"Do you think they will want to talk to us after all these years?"

"I believe they'll be happy to see us. I really miss them," Justin said.

"Me too."

"I'm sure they miss us too. At the end of the day, we're still family."

"You're right! So, how are we going to get in contact with them? I don't have their contact information, do you?" Jerome asked.

"No, but I'm sure they still attend Beautifully Blessed Christian Church…"

"So, that was the turning point and how we ended up at church," Jerome says.

"Well, I'm glad you guys decided to come to church. We have missed you both! We can never lose contact with each other again."

My brothers respond, "We won't!"

I look at the time and realize it's getting late. "Are you guys ready to go?

"Yes," they respond as we head for the door.

We get in my car and head to our destination.

Chapter Eight

"**W**hat exactly is the Building Better Men Program?" Justin asks.

"It's a mentoring program that's focused on helping young men in the community. The young men who attend this program have various behavior problems. Unfortunately, all of them come from single mother households. Pops used to be an elementary school teacher with the public school district. He saw a need for positive male role models in the community. So, he decided to start this program. They have a lot of professional volunteers like doctors, nurses, counselors, barbers, teachers, and lawyers. All the volunteers have provided donations over the years to help keep the program running. We also receive private donations. In the summer, the kids get to take field trips to amusement parks, water parks, and other places," I say as we pull into the parking lot of the program. "We're here." We get out the car and walk into the building towards Pops' office.

"Hi, Pops."

"Hey fellas." Pops shakes hands with Justin and Jerome.

"Hello again, sir."

"So, what are you guys up to today?"

"We're just hanging out. I thought it would be a good idea for them to see the program that helped me when I was younger," I say.

"Okay. Well, you guys can look around. I have a conference call in a few minutes."

"Thank, Pops!"

"Anytime."

Pops retreats into his office. I show Justin and Jerome around. "This program is staffed by positive educated men from all walks of life. The staff and volunteers are all drug and alcohol free. Also, they go through an extensive criminal background check. The students who have severe behavior problems are allowed to attend classes here. The young men do their schoolwork while learning how to handle their anger in a safe, positive environment. I spent majority of my days here. I hated being in regular schools and classrooms. This was the only place that I felt safe and comfortable. Also, it allowed me to receive some one-on-one assistance with my academics through the tutoring program. The best part is that I was surrounded by professional men who were genuinely concerned about my well-being. The young men are taught to be gentlemen. They attend group sessions that provide them an open forum. They are allowed to vent and discuss anything that is on their minds. And, it remains confidential."

"Sounds like it was a great program. Definitely would have been a big help to me growing up!" Jerome says.

"Man, always remember that everything happens for a reason. I know we wish all the trauma never happened. We can't focus on the negative aspects of it. It happened! Unfortunately, there's nothing we can do to undo it. Now, we must focus on moving forward. In order to do that, we must go through the necessary steps to heal. You have already started the process. It sounds like you are headed down the right track. Plus, Charity and I are here to help you."

"Yeah, things are going well. I have been thinking about joining your church and getting baptized. Life is short. I want to live and enjoy my life! I allowed Jada to ruin a good portion. I refuse to allow her to ruin the rest of it. When you are surrounded by people who want to make you as miserable as they are, it's hard to prevail. I'm ready to remove all negative energy from my surroundings. I don't want to go backwards anymore. I'm focused on moving forward. I no longer have the drugs and alcohol clouding my judgment. For the first time in a long time, I'm thinking with a clear mind."

"Jerome, I am so proud of you!"

"Me too. You have come a long way," Justin says.

"Yeah. I'm quite proud of myself and the direction that my life is headed!"

"Good for you, bro! Justin, did Jada ever try anything with you?"

"No, she never tried anything with me. I guess it was because I was rarely around her alone. I would come visit on the weekends. Since daddy was off on the weekends, she didn't have the opportunity to try anything."

"That makes sense. I was there all the time. So, she had plenty of opportunity, and she took full advantage of it! But, I don't want to think about her anymore."

"Understandable. Let's move to a happier topic… Justin, how are Simone and Serenity?"

"They're good. Serenity has finally gotten on a sleep schedule. For a while, she kept waking up every two hours for a bottle. Simone and I were exhausted. Simone's grandmother suggested we put cereal in her bottle because she wasn't getting full. So, we tried it. My wife gave her a bath at about 8:00 p.m. with some lavender bath gel. After her bath, she got her ready for bed and gave her a warm bottle with cereal. When she finished her bottle, my wife burped her, rocked her for a little bit, and she was out like a light," he laughs. "She sleeps the whole night until 6:00 a.m. now. We've been doing that routine ever since."

"I know you two are relieved."

"Yep. We couldn't rest with those feedings every two hours. Man, we both were super cranky," he laughs.

I laugh, too. "I bet. Those old school tricks always work!"

"Yes, they do. Now, we call her grandmother for everything. She's probably tired of us calling."

We all laugh.

"I'm sure she loves it!" I say.

Jerome asks, "Are you still planning to go with Charity to visit Daddy?"

"Yes, I'm going to see him. After talking to all of you, I figured it would be a good idea. We're leaving in the morning."

Justin asks, "Are you still angry at him?"

"No, I don't think I'm angry. I am still hurt though. His decision to bring Jada into our lives opened the doorway to abuse for us. He barely knew her. Yet, he allowed her to destroy our family."

"I don't think daddy would have allowed her into our lives if he knew the consequences of it," Justin says.

"That's the problem! He didn't take the time to think about the consequences of his actions. He saw a physically attractive woman with no children and freedom. Jada had no problem with him smoking weed, drinking, and staying out late with the fellas. Mama focused on structure for all of us. In his mind, the grass was greener on the other side."

"You're right! Daddy was wrong on so many levels and didn't see the damage until it was too late," Justin replies.

"I was in the house with him and Jada. He didn't see a lot of things. But, that's how Jada wanted it. It's like she had some kind of mind control over him. Daddy never acted like that with Desirae. And, your mom never mistreated us! Jaxxson, do you remember Timothy from down the street?"

"Yeah. Didn't his uncle move in with them?"

"Yep, Uncle Sly. I used to think that Desirae was mean for not letting us go play over Timothy's house. Now, I know she was just being a protective mother."

"What do you mean?" I ask.

"Well, shortly after Desirae and daddy divorced, Uncle Sly got arrested."

"For what?"

"Raping and attempted murder of Timothy! He ended up with several other charges on top of those," Jerome answers.

"What?! But, Uncle Sly was always chasing some woman. He was always bragging about all the women that he slept with."

Justin continues, "Yep, it was just a cover. After he raped him, Timothy threatened to tell. Well Uncle Sly didn't want everybody to know that he liked little boys. So, he beat Timothy so bad that he almost killed him. His mom had just gotten home from work when she heard Timothy screaming. She ran in the house and saw her brother beating him like a grown man! She tried to get him to stop but he wouldn't. So, she went and grabbed her gun from the bedroom drawer. When she came back in the room, he was still beating on Timothy. So, she shot him in the arm. She started asking what was going on and trying to help Timothy. The next-door neighbor, Caleb, heard the gunshot and came running over to check on everyone. At that moment, Timothy confessed that his uncle had raped him and wanted to keep him from telling."

"Wow. That's some crazy shit!" I say.

"Yep. With all the shit that happened to me and what happened to Timothy, I get it! Now, I understand that she was just trying to protect us. She knew what dangers were lurking in the world. She knew that it didn't have to be a stranger that could hurt us. It could be your own flesh and blood. Timothy's blood uncle raped him. Man, this shit just has me thinking a lot. I'm definitely more aware of people that are around me," Jerome says.

"Bro, I'm so sorry. Is Timothy, okay?

"Actually, I talked to him last week. He spent years in therapy, but he's good.

"I'm glad he is doing good. Unfortunately, parents don't always realize how their actions can affect their children," I say.

Justin adds, "No, they don't. I will definitely make a conscience effort with Serenity."

"Yeah. If I ever have children, I will as well.

"I don't plan on having children."

"Why not, Jerome?"

"I just don't see children in my future."

Justin responds, "You never know. Just because you don't see it now, doesn't mean that it's not a possibility later."

"Maybe. I still have a lot of healing to do before I can even think about being with a woman. Jada is the only woman that I have been with, and that experience has tormented me for years. I just don't have an interest in being with a woman romantically."

"I get it. I just recently got to the point where I wanted a romantic relationship with a woman. Once you're further along in your healing, it may become a possibility."

"Maybe. Only time will tell!"

"Justin, do you want to have more children?"

"Definitely. I think it's important for Serenity to have at least one sibling, but I'm not in a rush to make it happen now," he laughs.

I also laugh, "Man, I hear ya!"

Chapter Nine

A s I patiently wait for my turn to use the phone, I observe my current surroundings. There are men in orange jumpsuits with white socks and white slides, guards watching our every move, and gray walls. Our 6'x8' prison cells have the limited accommodations of a small cot, sheet, thin blanket, pillow, and toilet. The stainless-steel cell doors are controlled by guards in a secured observation booth. Armed guards are standing at every available post to ensure the inmates don't step out of line. I have been here for four months. I should be used to this place by now, but it feels like I've been in this hellhole forever. How did I ever get to this point? Every time I close my eyes, I pray that I'm just in a horrible dream. When I open my eyes, I'm still here... Finally, it's my turn to use the phone.. I pick up the receiver and dial.

"Hi, Daddy," my daughter responds.

"Hi, Princess! I've missed you so much."

"I missed you, too."

"I'm so sorry that I haven't been there for you and Jaxxson. Even though Desirae and I divorced, that should not have stopped me from being a father to you and Jaxxson. I would like to see you both."

"I would love to see to see you, too. Unfortunately, Jaxxson is still pretty upset with you."

"Yeah, I know. I handled that whole situation poorly. I really want the opportunity to explain. I'm going to call him later today," I say.

"Okay. I'll talk to Jaxxson. I'll work on convincing him to come for a visit in a few weeks."

"Thanks, princess! I love you, Charity!"

"I love you too, daddy!" She says and then hangs up.

I walk back to my cell after returning the receiver to the phone. Sadly, this is my primary connection to the outside world. It's hard to believe that four months ago, I was a free man. If someone would have told me ten years ago that I would be in jail for murdering my wife, I would have sworn that they were smoking some strong shit! I'm still surprised that I killed, Jada. There's no denying it, I did it! After hearing everything that Jerome told me that night, I couldn't let her continue to get away with it anymore. Not to mention, what she did to Jaxxson years ago. She had already gotten away with it far too long.

Jaxxson! I should have believed him. I didn't even consider the fact that he could have been telling the truth. I just brushed it off. I took Jada's word over my own child. Why didn't I listen? How could she abuse my boys? I have been an absent father from

Jaxxson's and Charity's lives for years. That was something that I never wanted to do to my children. My father walked out on my mom for another woman when I was thirteen years old, and I never heard from him again. Not a word! I swore that I would never be like him. But, it turns out that I'm exactly like him. Even though I will spend the rest of my life behind bars, I have to repair my relationship with Jaxxson and Charity. Jaxxson. I know this is never going to be an easy conversation, but I have to try. I walk back out to the common area for another phone call. Surprisingly, there isn't a line waiting to use to the phone. I pick up the receiver and dial another number.

"Hello?" his voice answers.

"Hey, son."

"Jayyson?"

"Yeah. How have you been, Jaxxson?"

"No, you don't get to do that! It's been fourteen years! Don't pretend to care about me now!" he yells.

"You're right! I'm sorry for that!"

"What do you want, Jayyson?"

"I want to see you, Jaxxson. I want a chance to explain."

"And what makes you think that I want to hear anything that you have to say?"

"Please Jaxxson! I know you're very angry with me. And you have every right to be angry. I just want a chance to explain," I plead.

"I'll think about it. Goodbye, Jayyson!"

Click. He hangs up, and I do the same. I knew that it wouldn't be easy, but I was hoping for a better reaction than that. He hates me. I think about how I messed up as I walk back to my cell again. Back to reality… I'm looking at the same gray walls inside my cell for the umpteenth time. I know I have to face the consequences of my actions, but how can I survive the rest of my life in this hell hole?

Life. My life has been on a downhill spiral since I cheated on Desirae with Jada. I've cheated before, but Desirae always forgave me. This time was different. When she found out about Jada, she shut down and wouldn't talk to me, cook for me, do my laundry, or even touch me. She stopped everything with me. On top of that, she took the kids and moved out. The next thing I know, I got served with divorce papers! I tried apologizing, sending flowers, and begging her to come home. Nothing worked! My world was shattered. I wanted my family back.

I slipped into a deep depression. I would call into work sick every day! When I ran out of sick days, I used vacation days. I never took time off before then, so I had plenty of time built up. My boss knew that I had some family problems, so he covered for me. He worked it out so that I wouldn't get terminated while I worked through my problems. I had literally hit rock bottom. One day my best friend, Greydon, showed up at my house. He called but I wouldn't answer the phone. He knocked on the doors and windows, but I still wouldn't answer. Finally, he remembered where I kept the spare key. He used the key to open the door and walked in. He saw me lying on the couch with beer bottles strewn all over the room. I was asleep, so he started shaking me.

"*Jayyson! Jayyson! Are you okay?*"

"*Huh…what…okay…*"

I woke up for a moment and drift back to sleep. He walked over to the kitchen sink. Got a glass and filled it with cold water. Then, he walked back over to me and poured the water on my face. I gasped.

"*What the heck! Why did you do that?*"

"*Get up, man! You have been sulking long enough! It's time to get back to life! Desirae is gone! She ain't coming back! I told you that shit was going to catch up to you!*" *he fussed.*

"*Really, bruh! This is not the time for I told you so!*"

"*Oh yes, it is! You need to hear it! I told you to stop cheating or she would get fed up! And that's exactly what happened! You made the decision to put sex before your family! Now, you have to live with it! Get the fuck up…*"

My daydream is interrupted as the guard shouts, "Lights out!"

As I am sitting on my cot, I begin thinking that I haven't been a very good friend to Greydon in a long, long time. Unfortunately, Jada put a strain on that relationship as well. I decide to write him a letter.

Dear Greydon,

    I am so sorry! I allowed Jada to destroy our relationship! You and I have always been more like brothers than best friends. But, from the moment that Jada came into the picture, our relationship began to deteriorate. Even when Sonja tried to tell me that Jada was cheating, I refused to believe it. Unfortunately, I have been blind to her manipulative ways for years.

    Obviously, I've had a lot of time to reflect over my life. I'm so disgusted at how it turned out. At one point in, my life was great. Desirae was the best thing that ever happened to me. She made me want to be a better man. For years, I did everything that I knew to be the best man possible for her and father to our children. But I was selfish! I started feeling like she wasn't giving me enough attention. That lack of attention led me back to my old ways. I failed!

    I hate that I destroyed my family. Jaxxson tried to tell me that Jada abused him. He was nine years old and had only been with us for two weeks. Jerome finally admitted that she had been abusing him for years. All this happened right under my nose. How did I miss it? I never imagined anything like this ever happening. How the hell could a grown woman think about sex with a child? That concept does not make any sense to me! How did I not see that she was using my boys for her own twisted sexual pleasure?

    I used to think that Desirae was being overprotective of the kids by not allowing them to sleep over to a friend's or family member's house. When the kids wanted to play outside, Desirae was right there watching them! She always watched adults and children around the kids. When Justin and Jerome were with us, she protected them the same way. She didn't play when it came to her children! Me on the other hand, I was always the laxed parent. I wanted them to be kids and have fun. I gave them a little more freedom than Desirae. I finally understand what caused her to be so protective. She wanted to make sure the kids never crossed paths with this type of danger.

I reached out to Charity and Jaxxson and asked them to come see me. As expected, Charity was very receptive. Jaxxson is a totally different story. He doesn't want anything to do with me. I should have expected that reaction, but I was hoping that he would have an open mind. Hopefully, Charity will be able to convince him to come. I really need to apologize to him in person. I want to repair my relationship with them both. Unfortunately, I will spend the rest of my life in prison. I really appreciate everything that you have done for me! I already know that you are working on delivering the letters that I wrote to the kids. I have a meeting scheduled with my lawyer, Chase Blankenship, to discuss the case. My main goal is to make sure what Jada did to Jerome and Jaxxson does not come out in the public. I failed in protecting them in the past. I don't want to fail them anymore. I love you, Greydon. We will always be brothers!

Sincerely,
Jayyson

Shit! I fucked up. I made the biggest mistake marrying Jada. I chose her over Desirae, Jaxxson, and Charity. What was I thinking? Desirae. I had the biggest crush on her in high school…

Chapter Ten

*A*s I walked into my sixth period Algebra class, I noticed this petite red bone with beautiful brown eyes. I was mesmerized. She had this shy, nerdy vibe about her. Me on the other hand, I was far from shy. I was smart but considered more of a class clown. There were many times when I would ask Desirae to help me with an assignment as an excuse to talk to her. I flirted with her constantly and asked her out almost every day. Each time, she shot me down.

"I know about your reputation with the ladies. I know the other ladies fall for the shit that you feed them, but I am not them! You are not going to manipulate me with your mind games just to get in my pants!"

She was the only one to ever reject me. Naturally, I took that as a personal challenge. I had to make her mine. I chased her all through high school but never got a date…until…three years after graduation…

I knocked on her door. "Who is it?" she answered.

"Jayyson with Just Cable."

She opened the door. "Jayyson?"

"Hi, Desirae!" We embraced in a brief friendly hug.

"Come in. How are you?"

"I'm good. How have you been?"

"I'm good," she said.

Suddenly, my phone rung. "It's work, excuse me. Hello…Yes, I'm here now…Okay, bye…Sorry about that."

"No problem."

I stuck to business even though my heart was pounding from excitement. "Where do you want your cable?"

"Here in the living room and there in the bedroom."

"Okay. Well, let me get to work."

While I working, she continued preparing dinner in the kitchen. I got her cable setup in about thirty minutes. Then, I showed her that everything is ready to go.

"What are you cooking?" I asked.

"Lasagna."

"It sure smells good."

"Would you like some dinner? Or, do you need to go to your next job?" she offered.

"That was my supervisor on the phone. My last two jobs cancelled. And, I'm off for the weekend."

She smiled. "Great! You can use the restroom to wash up." Then, she fixed our plates and set them on the table. "What do you want to drink? Bottled water or soda?"

"Bottled water is fine." I closed out the job on my work app and then we sat down at the dining room table and begin catching up between bites. I told her about my job and my children. Justin was two years old, and Jerome was just a year old.

"Things didn't work out with their mothers, but I am very active in my boys' lives."

"It's good that you are active in their lives," she said.

"Yeah. So, what have you been up to these days?"

"I'm working to finish my degree in Human Resources at Higher Achievement University. I currently work as an HR Clerk at Sunshine Telecommunications."

"That's good. What about your social life? Are you seeing anyone?" I asked.

"No social life. School and work are it. Are you seeing anyone?"

"No."

She smiled and replied, "That's a surprise!"

"Why do you say that?" I quiz.

"As I recall, you kept multiple girls when we were in high school."

I laughed. "Yeah, but that only got me into trouble."

"I know."

We both laughed.

"Are you finished with your plate?" she asked.

"Yes. That was delicious."

"Thank you."

"You're welcome." She started cleaning up the kitchen.

"Would you like some help?" I offered.

"No, I've got it. You're a guest. Do you want to watch a movie?"

"Yes," I gladly said.

She handed me the remote and asked me to find something to watch. As she finished in the kitchen, I searched the guide channel.

"Do you want to watch this?" I asked.

After finishing in the kitchen, she walked in the living room. She looked at the TV and says, "Yes."

We sat on the couch to watch the movie. As time went on, I put my arm around her shoulder. Surprisingly, she didn't reject me.

"I have had a crush on you for a very long time," I admitted.

"I know. You weren't exactly known to be with one woman."

"True. If you give me a chance, I would love to be faithful to you."

Blushing, she said, "I'll think about it. Friends first. If a relationship develops, great. If not, we remain friends. Agreed?"

"Agreed. Can I take you out on a date tomorrow as a friend?"

"That'll be fine," she accepted.

We continued watching the rest of the movie in silence. "I would love to stay longer, but I'm picking up my boys in the morning." I got up to leave. "Is seven o'clock a good time for you?"

She walked me to the door. "Yes. I will be ready."

We embraced in a hug. I bent down to kiss her, but she turned her head. My kiss landed on her cheek.

"Friends first!" she reminded me.

"You can't blame me for trying!" I laughed slightly.

"Goodnight, Jayyson."

"Goodnight, Desirae..."

The next day, I arrived a few minutes before our scheduled date and knocked on her door.

"Who is it?"

"Jayyson."

Desirae opened the door. "Hi, Jayyson. Come in."

She had on a short sleeveless navy blue dress with yellow open toe heels and accessories to match. Her hair was up in a neat bun. No makeup, only clear lip gloss.

"Wow. You look beautiful!" I blushed.

"Thank you."

I handed her a bouquet of yellow roses.

"These are beautiful. Thank you."

She smiled and sniffed the roses.

I returned the smile. "You're welcome."

"Have a seat. Let me put these in some water."

I couldn't help but watch her every step. She headed to the kitchen and grabbed a clear vase from the counter. She filled it with water and placed the roses in it. Then, she set the vase on the dining room table. That's when she noticed me watching.

"Is something wrong?"

I was slightly embarrassed, but I didn't let it show. "Not at all. I'm just admiring the view."

She blushed and grabbed her purse. Then, she locked the door as we headed out. I took her hand and guided her to my car.

"*So, where are we going tonight?*"

I opened her door and waited for her to get in the car. "*It's a surprise!*" I closed her door and walked around to my side of the car.

"*I love surprises,*" she said as I drove to our destination.

"*Good.*"

"*What did you and the boys do today?*"

"*We went to Sea Swift Park. They played on the playground slide, merry go round, swings, and sandbox. And, they played in the kiddie pool. Then, I took them to get something to eat.*"

She smiled. "*I bet they had a good time. And, I'm sure they were exhausted by the time you took them home.*"

Laughing, I replied, "*Yep. They were knocked out before I turned the corner after eating.*"

"*It's good that you make time for your boys.*"

"*I love being a dad. My boys are some cool kids,*" I said as I turned into the parking lot. "*We're here!*"

"*Kamz Lounge?*" she said as she looked around.

"*Yeah. Do you still like spoken word?*"

"*Yes. How did you know?*"

"*How could I forget? I remember you were always carrying around a book of poetry in school. Anytime you had a thought, you would write it down. And, you allowed me to read one of your poems after your brother passed away.*"

"*Really? You remember that?*" she asked.

"*It was called 'The Pain Behind My Smile.'*" I recited the poem.

"The pain behind my smile is so severe
That I struggle every day to see things clear.

I put on a smile like everything is alright
But I am so filled with darkness, that there is very
little light.

The pain behind my smile creates dark clouds
And I really want to scream and yell out loud.

The pain behind my smile is so fresh and clear
I have never in my life, shed so many tears.

I cannot pretend to be unbothered by your journey to
heaven
So, I'm speaking my truth, this is my confession.

The pain behind my smile will eventually fade away
In the meantime, the pain behind my smile is here to
stay!"

Desirae had tears in her eyes. "I'm surprised you
remembered."
"That was the first time you allowed me to be a
friend. I wanted to be with you from the first moment I saw
you."
"I know. But, you were way too focused on getting
into my pants. If that is what you are expecting to happen
now, you're sadly mistaken!" she advised.

"No, that's not what I've been thinking. Yes. I got plenty of girls back in the day. I'm a grown man now. I want a woman. A woman that has more to offer than sex. She'll be my friend before anything. Someone that I can invest in, and she can invest in me. Someone that I can build a future with while we're helping each other grow!"

I got out the car and walked over to her side. Then, I opened her door and helped her out of the car.

"I want to be faithful to you. I'm perfectly fine with being friends first."

She just smiled. "We shall see! Do you come here often?"

"I recently started coming here. Actually, I was hoping to run into you. It's an open mic lounge for various artists to showcase their talents. Tonight is for poets."

Kamz Lounge is an orange building with graffiti art decorating the walls. The inside reflects the same graffiti art on an orange background. There was a young lady dressed in all black standing at a podium near the front door. We sat at a booth near the stage as a guy walked up to the mic. The guy was short with curly black and gray hair and brown skin. He wore black framed glasses, baggy jeans, and a plain white t-shirt. He had a very energetic vibe.

"Good evening, everyone. I'm your MC Zolie. Next up, we have Precious Wordz."

Precious Wordz was a short plus-sized beauty with dark brown skin and brown eyes. She had box braids that were twisted into a neat bun. She was wearing a baby blue crop top with high waisted denim jeans, and baby blue heels.

"Hello, everyone. I'm Precious Wordz…

Suffer in Silence

Why do you think it is normal to hurt me until I
concede?
It's like you find ultimate pleasure out of making me
bleed!

I was blamed for the miscarriage in the summer of
last June
But it was the result of you leaving me all bloody and
bruised.

Why am I constantly made to feel worthless through
sheer misery?

Yet, all of this mistreatment is because of your
insecurities.

The words no man will ever want you invade my
thoughts on a daily

I have no friends, no family; there is no one around to
help save me.

As I contemplate leaving, I stare at the fresh blood on
my dinner plate

But this just might be the final straw towards sealing
my fate!

I suffer in silence because that's what I have been
conditioned to do

But how much longer will it take for me to finally
reach my breakthrough!"

Finger snaps erupted throughout the audience.
Zolie stepped back to the mic and said, "That was Precious
Wordz. Let's welcome Genesis Rayne to the stage."
Again, finger snaps erupt throughout the audience.
Genesis Rayne was a slim, short lady with smooth caramel
skin and dark brown eyes. She had brown hair that was in a
halo braid, and she was wearing a white baby doll t-shirt,
skinny jeans, and white wedge sandals.

"Good evening, everyone. As Zolie stated, my
name is Genesis Rayne. I have been on a long journey
of healing. I want to recite a poem that is very
personal to me…

Scars

A rainbow of colors cover me, and no one has a clue
But the predominant colors that I see are black and
blue.

I use makeup and dark clothing to hide the bruises
with skill

Until recently, my lips have always remained sealed.

I live in constant fear of being slapped, punched, or kicked
Why? Oh Why, did I ever get hitched?

Bitch, slut, hoe are hurled at me so often
I wonder constantly, if I will end up in a coffin.

I think of yelling and running out the door, past his fields
But memories of past encounters, cause me to yield.

All the wounds and bruises have all been concealed
Just because you don't see them, doesn't mean that my scars have healed!"

The crowd erupted with finger snaps of approval.
Desirae said, "Both poems were powerful. Sadly, I can imagine the pain that they must have endured."
"Yeah, but for them to be up there speaking about it sounds like they are no longer in that situation."
"Thank you for bringing me here. I am really having a good time with you," she said.
"You're welcome. I'm having a good time with you. I wanted to show you that I'm serious about being with you," I said.
"You did a good job. It's only the first date though. Don't get ahead of yourself."

I laughed. "Would you like something to eat or drink?"

"No, I'm content for the moment," she said.

"Let me know if you change your mind."

"I will. So…other than spend time with your boys, what else do you do in your spare time?

"Nothing really. Every once in a blue moon, I go to Denica's Pool Lounge to shoot pool. Primarily, I'm spending time with my boys."

She smiled. "That's good. I have never been one for the social scene, but I have always wanted to learn how to shoot pool. Can you teach me?"

I returned the smile. "I would love to teach you. I want to spend a lot of time with you. Sometimes, we can go out. Sometimes, we can stay inside. At some point down the line, I would love for you to meet my boys."

"We will see how things go…"

I'm awakened from my dream at the sound of my name being called. The guard shouts, "Craig! Craig, wake up! Your attorney is here to see you."

I get up as the guard is signaling to open my cell. I walk towards him. He shackles my hands and escorts me to a secured steel room away from the other inmates. The room has a steel table and stool seats bolted to the ground and wall. He links my shackles to a bar on the table. My attorney, Chase Blankenship, is already waiting.

"Good morning, Mr. Craig. How are you feeling this morning?"

"Good morning, Mr. Blankenship. The same. I hate being here. I would prefer to be home, but I know that will never happen. Did you get an update on my plea agreement?"

"Yes. I met with Prosecuting Attorney Shelbi Blacke a few days ago. She has agreed to offer you a plea agreement of life in prison without the possibility of parole. In exchange, you must tell us everything that happened prior to, during, and after the murder of your wife, Jada LeShay Craig."

"What about the other part?" I ask.

"She has agreed to keep the abuse of Jaxxson Craig and Jerome Craig out of the public eye."

"Are you sure? It is very important that the abuse is not made public. I failed to protect my boys in the past. I do not want their personal business in the news."

"I understand, Mr. Craig. She has assured me that it will not be disclosed to the public."

"Perfect!" I sigh.

"We have a meeting scheduled next week. In the meeting, you are to disclose everything surrounding the death of your wife. The Prosecuting Attorney, court recorder, and I will be in attendance. The court recorder will document your statement word for word to generate your signed confession."

"I understand. Thank you, Mr. Blankenship."

"You're welcome, Mr. Craig. I will see you next week." Mr. Blankenship rises and leaves the room.

The guard enters the room an unlinks my shackles from the bar on the table and escorts me back to my cell.

Chapter Eleven

"Jaxx, are you sure you don't want me to drive? We have a two-hour ride ahead of us to E.L.W. Prison."

"Yes, I'm sure," I say to my sister.

"Are you nervous?"

"A little. You?"

"A lot! This is the first time that we've seen Jayyson since we were kids."

"I'm sure it'll be fine, Charity."

"Jaxxson?"

"Yes?"

"Are you okay?" she asks.

"Yes. Why do you ask?"

"Because you're way too calm right now." Whispering, she adds, "Have you been smoking?"

Laughing, I reply, "No, I haven't been smoking. Have you?"

"No, I haven't. I'm just saying you are little too calm right now. I would think that you would be a nervous wreck," she laughs.

"I'm good, Charity! I'm just trying not to expect too much out of this visit. I think the letters that Jayyson wrote us helped. Plus, reconnecting with

Justin and Jerome has been a bonus. I have truly enjoyed having my big brothers back in my life. It's sad that it took all this bad stuff for us to get to this point."

"Yeah, and I really hate that you and Jerome suffered the abuse."

I sigh. "Unfortunately, Jerome suffered a lot more than I did. He endured years of abuse from Jada, and it almost destroyed him. It took a lot of courage for him to speak up. I know telling Jayyson was not easy. He has a long journey of recovery ahead of him…but…he is headed in the right direction."

"Yeah! I'm glad that he finally spoke up. His life is finally on the right track!"

Smiling, I say, "Yeah. I'm so proud of him!

She smiles too and says, "I'm proud of both of you! The devil tried his best to knock you down, but you didn't give up. You kept going. There's so much growth from both of you!"

"We are still growing, but I'm excited for the direction our growth is taking us."

"So, you know that I have to ask…how is Leah?"

Smiling, I say, "She's good. She called this morning to wish us good luck with seeing Jayyson."

"She is so sweet. I'm glad you finally started dating," Charity says.

"We've only been on a few dates. We're taking our time. We're still getting to know each other. She agreed that it's important to be friends first.

"But you like her right?"

"Yeah, I like her. She's an amazing young lady. We spent hours just talking about life. No lies, no games, and no drama. We are completely honest with each other about everything," I say with a smile.

"Aaawww."

"What?"

"It's good to see you happy, Jaxx."

"It's good to be happy! So, what about you and what's his face?"

"Who? Tony?" Charity says.

"Yeah, Tony!"

"There is no more Tony!"

"Why? What happened?"

"We went out on a couple dates but no real chemistry. There was no reason to waste any more time with him. My friend, Sienna, wants me to go out with her brother, but I'm not sure if it will work," she says.

"Why?"

"Suppose I go out with him and it's awful! It could jeopardize my relationship with Sienna."

I reply, "But, what if the date goes great?"

"Yeah but…"

"But nothing. Give the man a shot! Wait…what does he do?"

"Actually, he owns the Red Bottom Galore Restaurant downtown."

"A businessman. That's good. Baby Mama drama? Stalker ex?"

She says, "No and no."

"Alright! So, give the man a chance. You don't have to marry him tomorrow. Go out with him. You might have a good time."

"Alright, Jaxx! I will give him a chance! Thanks little big bro."

"Anytime! Well, it looks like we're here," I say.

We drive up to a two-story concrete gray building surrounded by a high chain link fence with razor, barbed wire at the top. Armed guards are in the observation towers and around the perimeter of the prison. We follow the signs to the visitor parking on the North side of the building. We are greeted by guards as we walk into the visitor's entrance. They ask for our driver's licenses and the name of the inmate that we are visiting. They compare our information to the visitor's log sheet. Next, we're asked to take everything out of our pockets and place them in a bowl on the table. Then, we are told to walk through the metal detectors one at a time.

Once we are cleared for entry, the guards escort us to the visitation room. It's a large plain room with gray walls just like the outside of the building. There are plain white round tables with four plastic chairs surrounding each of them. The tables and chairs are spaced out throughout the room. The inmates are escorted into the room in a single file line. Once all the inmates are seated at different tables, we are allowed to go to our corresponding inmate. We noticed Jayyson as soon as he walked into the room. He looks slightly different from what I remember, but the features are still there. He has gotten so frail with all the weight loss. His low-cut afro and goatee have turned completely gray. The wrinkles on his face have aged him by ten years. Jayyson displays a huge smile on his face as he spots us walking in his direction.

"Jaxxson. Charity. Thank you for coming to visit."

"No problem."

"Charity, you have grown into a beautiful young lady."

"Thank you, daddy."

"Jaxxson, you are a handsome young man. You look just like me in my younger days."

"Yeah, I know. So, what did you want to talk to us about?" I say.

"Jaxxson." Charity slaps my shoulder.

"It's okay. I know I let you down, Jaxxson. I've let a lot of people down. I am so sorry that I didn't believe you. I should have done a better job of protecting you…Jerome…our family."

"Yes, you should have done a better job!"

"I know, Jaxxson. Unfortunately, I can't change the past, but I would like to repair my relationship with you and Charity now."

He looks at Charity and says, "Sweetheart, I am so sorry!"

"I know, daddy. We talked to Jerome, and he told us everything. Everything that Jada did to him!"

"Yeah. I promise I had no idea what was happening. That shit has never happened in my family."

"That you know of… I'm sure your family didn't tell you everything that went on behind closed doors. Family secrets… Stop saying it has never happened in your family. It has happened in your family! It happened to Jerome and me under your nose!"

"You're right, Jaxxson," he says.

"Daddy, if you cared so much about us, why didn't you reach out to see us?" Charity asks.

"Pride. I never stopped loving you and Jaxxson. I thought about you every day over the years. I wanted to call, but I knew Desirae wouldn't allow me back into your lives."

"Can you blame her? She trusted you with her children. You knew how protective she was over us and why she was that way. Why didn't you take those same protective measures? You left Jerome and me alone with a pedophile. She raped us on numerous occasions. I told you when it happened. You didn't believe me. You took her word over mine," I say firmly.

"No, I can't blame Desirae. I didn't see what was happening. I didn't want to hear what you were telling me. Yes, I should have listened. I should have known that you were telling the truth back then. It just didn't seem real! When Jerome told me, that's when it became real!"

"It should have been real when it came out of Jaxxson's mouth, daddy!" Charity splutters.

"You're right, Charity. It should have been real when Jaxxson told me, but it wasn't. I know I should have handled that situation completely different. I can't change my actions back then. There is nothing that I can say to you that will change it. After Jerome told me what had been happening to him for years, I snapped! I knew he was telling the truth. And, I knew that you were telling the truth all those years ago. So, I had to figure out the best way to stop her.

"Yes, I could have just called the cops and reported it, but I didn't want to take the chance of her getting away with it anymore! I wanted to make sure she wasn't able to hurt anyone else ever again! The only way that I knew to do that was to kill her. Now, I will spend the rest of my life in prison. I thought about committing suicide after I killed her…"

"Why didn't you? Mama told us that you used to call her during your depressed moments talking about suicide," Charity asks.

"I did, Charity. I called her because she was the only person who I could really express my feelings. I know I messed up! I regretted my choice of Jada over Desirae for years. I wanted to get back with Desirae. I tried multiple times. Because I cheated, she never trusted me again. I didn't want to be by myself, so I stayed with Jada."

"So, you settled?" I ask.

"Yes."

"If Mama was the one that you really wanted, why did you cheat on her in the first place?"

He says, "Stupid! We were having some problems, and I started to feel neglected. By the time I would get home from work, Desirae never had time for me. She was always tired."

"She was tired!" Charity says. "She worked a regular full-time job, she was a full-time mother, and she helped us with homework. She cooked dinner and made sure we were fed, she ironed our school clothes for the next day, and she cleaned house while we took our baths. Plus, she did what she needed to do for herself. All that was before you got home from work at night. There were many times when we went to bed before you even got home from work. Did you even consider everything that she did during the day?"

"No, I didn't. I was getting more attention from other women than my own wife. So, I felt like she didn't want to be with me anymore."

Charity added, "As your wife and mother of your children, Mama had a lot more responsibilities! She may not have been giving you the attention that you wanted, but she loved you! The other women didn't give a damn about you! They were flirting and showing interest because they wanted to sleep with you. Plain and simple. You gave up love for lust! You jeopardized our family for a temporary fix. Your choice to settle for Jada caused a lot of harm to Jaxxson and Jerome. They have spent years trying to heal from it! You didn't even think about how your actions would affect your children!"

"You're right, Charity. I just didn't see it like that at the time. And, I definitely didn't consider the consequences of my actions."

"No, you didn't! The only reason you see it now is because of your current situation. I'm sure you've had a lot of time to think," she continues.

"Yes, Charity. I've had a lot of time to think about my life and the choices I made over the years. I know that I have to live with the consequences of my actions. And, I'm prepared to do that. I would like to restore my relationships with you and Jaxxson. Hopefully, Justin and Jerome will allow me the opportunity to repair my relationship with them."

"I'm here today, but I cannot guarantee that I will continue to visit," I say.

"I'm not sure either, daddy. I think it will take some time before Justin and Jerome will even consider coming to see you."

"I understand. If this is the only time that I get to see or talk to you, I will have to accept it. I really appreciate you both for coming today. If Justin and Jerome decide to keep their distance, I will have to accept that as well."

"We will play it by ear, daddy. I will let them know that you want to see them. No guarantees though," she says.

"Thank you, princess! I spoke to my attorney the other day. He is working on a plea agreement with the Prosecuting Attorney. I have to disclose everything surrounding Jada's murder. In exchange, I get life in prison without the possibility of parole. And, she has agreed to keep Jaxxson and Jerome's abuse out of the public."

"Really?" I say.

"Yes, I failed you and your brother in the past. I wanted to do something right. I wanted to make sure your personal business doesn't get out."

"Personal business, seriously? You just don't want the world to know that your wife was fucking two of your boys! From the moment you got with Jada, you turned into a different person. You went from being a strong, dedicated family man to a weak excuse of a man. You barely knew Jada. You only knew the side that she wanted you to see!" I say.

Charity touches my hand as I continue. "You left her alone with your children. And, what did she do? She tortured them! She raped them! I told you! I told you and you didn't believe me. You think that just because you killed Jada after Jerome told you, that makes it okay? Well, it doesn't! Do you know the damage that shit caused me... Charity... Mama? There were times that I hated myself. I hated Jada! And, I hated you! I wondered if all this was my fault.

But it wasn't... This was your fault for bringing Jada into our lives. You were supposed to protect me! Why was that so hard for you to do?" I fight back tears.

"I don't know, Jaxxson. You're right. I did change into a different man with Jada. When my dad walked out on us, I was devastated. I swore that I would never do that to my family. But, I did! I did the same thing. I am no better than he was. I'm truly sorry for bringing Jada into our lives."

"I know you were hoping to repair our relationship, but I'm not sure if it can be repaired. I thought it could but seeing you after all these years and you're just sitting here like everything is good. It's not!"

The guard announces, "Visiting hours have, ended. Visitors, please remain seated while we secure the inmates. Inmates, form a line behind Officer Maddox."

He directs them to the inmate exit towards the back of the room.

As Jayyson prepares to leave, he whispers, "I love you, Charity! I love you, Jaxxson!"

The inmates do as they are instructed and are escorted out of the room.

The guard says, "Visitors, you may proceed to the visitor's exit."

We proceed to the exit and get into my car. We ride in silence for what seems like an eternity.

"Are you okay, Charity?"

"Yes, I'm okay. I didn't mean to blow up at Jayyson. He just made me so mad! He made it seem like Mama was neglecting him because she was tired. Like being tired was just some excuse for him to cheat. You saw all the work she had to do for us. Most of the time, he was at work. Everything was on her shoulders. Of course, she was tired!" she says.

"I understand. I didn't mean to blow up at him either. That visit took more energy than I expected.

"I agree. I feel drained."

I admit, "I'm not sure if I want to attempt this visit again."

Chapter Twelve

Chase Blankenship says, "Mr. Craig, are you ready?"

"Yes, I'm ready."

"As previously discussed, you must tell us everything surrounding the death of your wife, Jada LeShay Craig. In exchange, you will receive a life in prison sentence without the possibility of parole. Also, you are to disclose the abuse of Jaxxson Craig and Jerome Craig for documentation purposes to show your reasoning and rationale for killing your wife. As agreed upon, the abuse of Jaxxson Craig and Jerome Craig will remain out of the public. For the record, Prosecuting Attorney Shelbi Blacke, court recorder Jessica Smyth, Jayyson Craig, and myself, Defense Attorney Chase Blankenship are in attendance for this meeting. Do you have any questions before we begin?"

"No sir. I understand."

"Okay. You can begin whenever you are ready."

"It started when I called my best friend, Greydon James..." I recall the conversation.

"Greydon, what's up?"

"Nothing much. Date night with Sonja. What you gettin' into tonight?"

"Nothing much. Shootin' the shit with Justin and Jerome. The usual."

"That's cool. Well, let me get ready. I'll talk to you later."

Greydon hung up the phone. He's been my best friend for twenty-five years. We used to be more like brothers until I married Jada. We still talk every now and then, but it's not like it used to be. My phone rung and I answered it.

"Hey daddy."

"Hey Justin. What's up?"

"We already got the pizza and wings. Do you need us to get anything else?"

"No, I think that's everything," I said.

"Okay. We're coming down the street."

After a few moments, there was a knock on the door, and I answered it.

"Hey guys," I said. We embraced as they entered the house. "Do y'all want a beer?"

Jerome responded, "Yes."

"I have some in the cooler on the deck." We headed out back and had a seat. "So, what's been going on, Justin?" I asked.

"The usual. Just been working, trying to get as much overtime as possible. Simone had her thirty-week checkup today. Baby Serenity Simone Craig is growing on *schedule. I want to make sure that when she arrives, I can take a couple weeks off work," he beamed.*

"I can't wait to meet my grandbaby. Jerome, what's going on with you and the case?"

"It's going! I'm meeting with my lawyer in a couple days to see what my options are at this point. Other than that, just working and trying to stay out of trouble. Seems like every time I turn around, I'm in trouble for something. Constant bad luck! It's like the weight of the world is always on my shoulders."

Jerome had already finished one beer. He opened another and took a few drinks.

"Bro, don't say that! I'm sure it feels like that, but sometimes you have to just dance in the rain. You've had some bad breaks since you were little, but you have some blessings coming your way soon!" Justin said.

"Since I was little!" Jerome took a few more sips. Yeah, that's when it started. You know, I wish that I could go back in time. It never would've happened. And, my life wouldn't be so messed up!" Jerome's eyes were tearing up as he finished his second beer and started on another one.

Justin asked, "What happened when you were little?"

"I can't tell you!"

Jerome took a few more drinks.

"Bro, you can tell me anything! Speak your peace! What happened, Jerome?"

"Jada!" Jerome took a few more drinks. "Jada fucked up my childhood...my life!"

"Son, what are you talking about? What happened?" I asked.

Jerome's tears were flowing. Justin and I walked over to try to console him, but he backed away.

"Do you remember that time daddy was working, and we were home with Jada? I was nine years old, and you were ten years old. Jada sent you outside to play, but I had to stay inside to help her with something."

"Ah yeah, I remember. I thought it was weird because I offered to help but she insisted that I go outside to play."

"Yeah, I had to help her with something alright!" Jerome said as he finished his third beer.

"Okay. Tell us," Justin said.

"Jada told me that she has a special surprise for me. I thought it was a toy or ice cream. You know, something like that. After you went outside, she told me to come in the living room and have a seat on the couch. So, I did. On the TV, there was a naked man and woman. The man was sitting on the bed, but the woman was facedown between his legs. It was porn! Of course, I didn't know that at the time."

Justin shouted, "That bitch!"

"She started unzipping my pants and pulled my dick out. I tried to get up, but she made me sit back down."

She said, "Just keep watching TV. Then, she started rubbing on me. The next thing I know, she had it in in her mouth. I'm sure you can imagine what happened next. I was nine years old, and I had never had anything like that happen to me. It felt good but weird at the same time. I felt *so ashamed and embarrassed. When she finished, she zipped my pants up and told me this was our little secret. Daddy, she told me that I couldn't tell you because you would blame me."*

I responded, *"What the fuck!*

"That was the first time something like that happened, but it was definitely not the last. I realize now that she had been grooming me for a while before that happened."

"Grooming you? What do you mean, bro?"

"Since I spent most of my time with her while daddy was at work, she had a lot of uninterrupted opportunities. At first, her lingerie was always covered with her bathrobe. All of a sudden, she started walking around without the bathrobe. She would always find a reason to bend over in front of me to show her ass! She would give me hugs but made sure my face was in between her breasts.

"One day, she wanted me to get a drink from the refrigerator and bring it to her upstairs. I walked in on her while she was playing with herself! I apologized for not knocking on the door before entering, but she said it was okay and continued doing it. I put the drink down on the nightstand and ran out of the room. I was confused about what I saw but I was scared to tell you."

"Why would you be scared to tell me? That's some shit that you should have definitely told me!" I said.

"Every time someone tried to tell you anything about Jada that you didn't want to hear, you brushed it off or blamed that person!"

"No, I haven't!" I defended.

Jerome said, *"Yes, you have daddy! Remember when Greydon's girlfriend, Sonja, mentioned she saw Jada at Roundtree Park holding hands with some guy? You didn't believe it, but you asked Jada about it. She gave you some excuse about it being some childhood family friend. You brushed it off! What about the last time cousin DoLo came over? He was sleep on the couch. He woke up to find Jada giving him a blowjob! He cursed her out, pushed her away, and started yelling for you. He told you the truth about what happened, but Jada flipped the script! She accused him of making a pass at her.*

"You went off on DoLo for making a pass at your wife. Then, you kicked him out of the house and haven't spoken to him since it happened. You never believed anything against Jada. I told her months ago that I couldn't do it anymore! Haven't you noticed that I don't come over as much? And, when I do come, I make sure she is not here."

"Yeah, I noticed. I just figured you didn't want to be questioned about the case," I said.

"No, she is the reason! She is the reason my life is so fucked up! This is the reason why I'm always high or drunk! I didn't want to keep thinking about it! I wanted to do anything that I could to help me forget! I wanted to tell you when Jaxxson told you what she did to him, but you didn't believe him either."

"Wait, Jaxxson? Daddy, what happened to Jaxxson?" Justin asked.

I took a deep breath. "When Jaxxson was nine years old, he told me that Jada bit him in his private area. He said, she made him kiss her and it tasted nasty. Also, that she was on top of him."

"Jaxxson, said what?"

"Justin, I thought he was making it up. He was always saying he wanted me and Desirae back together."

"What the fuck! Let me get this straight: Jaxxson tells you that your WIFE bit him in his private area; she made him kiss her and it tasted nasty; and she was on top of him! You didn't do anything because you thought he was making it up so that you and Desirae could get back together! That is the dumbest shit I have ever heard! Daddy, what kid would make up some shit like that? Jaxxson was nine years old. Nine-year-old little boys are thinking about toy cars and action figures. Kids wouldn't know anything about sex unless it was introduced to them!"

"Justin, I never imagined that something like this would happen."

"Wait! Is this the real reason that we don't have a relationship with Jaxxson and Charity?" he asked.

I hung my head low and responded, "Yes."

"Wow. You told me that Desirae was keeping them from coming around us. That she refused to answer the phone anytime you called to get them. I can't believe you! You just brushed it off like it was no big deal! You don't just all of a sudden wake up one day and decide to do some shit like that to a kid. I guarantee there are other kids that she has done this to out there. I can't even look at you right

*now! This shit was going on under your nose! In your
house! And you did absolutely nothing about it?"*

"I didn't know! This shit has never happened in my
family. This shit would have never crossed my mind in a
million years," I said.

"The moment it came out of your son's mouth, you
should have done something! Ask questions…
investigate… something! You took the word of a pedophile
bitch over your flesh and blood! Who does that?"

"You're right! I shouldn't have ignored all the red
flags over the years. Jerome, I know there are no words that
can undo all the pain and hurt that you have experienced.
I'm so sorry that I brought Jada into our lives. I'm sorry
that I have been blind for so long. I promise that nothing
like this will ever happen again!"

Justin was infuriated. "Daddy, what have you
always told us? Accept yo' shit! It's time for you to take
your own advice. As far as I'm concerned, you are just as
much to blame as Jada! What kind of man doesn't believe
his own child? Jerome has been getting into trouble for
years! This explains it! I love you, but I don't want
anything else to do with you! I'm going to be there for my
brother! And, we're going to reconnect with Jaxxson and
Charily. This will be the last time you hear from us! Come
on, Jerome!"

They walked to the front of the house towards their
car. I followed behind them.

"Don't leave like this, Justin! Jerome! I know I
fucked up! I promise that I will make this right! Jada won't
hurt anyone else, ever again!"

They left me standing there. Eventually, I walked back into the house and had a beer. As I sat there, the events from the evening were on repeat in my mind. I spent the next forty-eight hours drinking beers and chain-smoking cigarettes. I was experiencing a rollercoaster of emotions. My own wife raped my boys! How the hell did I not see what was happening right in front of me? At that point, I debated turning her in to the police. But, I didn't want to take a chance of her going free because of some loophole. She had already gotten away with it for far too long. I wanted her to suffer for what she did to my sons. She had to pay...

When she Jada returned home, she said, "Hey baby!" and kissed me.

"Hey baby!" I replied like nothing was wrong.

"I am so glad to be home. I love my family, but they get on my last nerve."

"That bad, huh?" I asked.

"Yes, a lot of drama."

"Well, you're home now. Here, let me get your bags."

"Thank you, baby!"

"No problem. Come on into the kitchen, I have a surprise for you."

"Ooohhh, I love surprises."

"I know. I figured that you would be tired and hungry from traveling. So, I made dinner."

She smiled. "Aaawww, that's so sweet!"

"Have a seat." I pulled out her chair and let her sit down.

"So, what's on the menu?"

"Your favorite, Blackened Salmon with grilled shrimp in a cream sauce, grilled asparagus, loaded baked potatoes, dinner rolls, and a little red wine to wash it down," I forced a smile.

"This looks great!" She raised her glass preparing to take a drink.

I stopped her. "Wait, let's make a toast."

"To what?"

"To you, Jada LeShay Craig. I thought I would do something that shows my true feelings for you."

"Aaawww, Jayyson."

"This is just the beginning!" I said with a smile.

"Oh, really?" She smiled from ear to ear with excitement.

"Yes, really! I have a very special surprise for you after dinner."

"You really did miss me, huh?"

"You have no idea!" We ate dinner.

"So, what did you do while I was gone?"

"Just chilled, watched the game, drank a few beers, and thought about you."

"What about me?"

"Just some things that I wanted to do to you when you got home," I said.

Smiling, she asked, "Like what?"

"Nice try!"

"Not even a little hint?" She pouted.

"Stop pouting. You will see in due time."

She finished her meal and wiped her mouth with her napkin. "Dinner was delicious, baby!"

"Thanks! Do you want some dessert? I made German Chocolate cake."

"That sounds good, but I am stuffed."

"Are you sure?"

"Yes, maybe later," she said.

"Okay. Let me clear the table." I got up and put our dirty dishes in the sink.

"Can I have my surprise now?"

"Not yet," I said.

"Why not?"

"Because it's not time yet."

With a sad face, she said, "Okay."

"Don't be disappointed. Have a little patience."

"You're right!"

"Why don't you come talk to me while I clean the kitchen?" I said.

"What do you want to talk about?"

"Hhhmmm, let me think. I got it! Do you remember the night that we met?"

Smiling, she replied, "Of course! How could I forget? Miyanna and I needed to get out the house. So, we decided to go to Spiralz Sports Bar. We sat at one of the booths near the pool tables." She paused and laughed. "We wanted to check out the men. We ordered some drinks and wings. That's when I saw this tall, sexy chocolate you, of course! You were with Greydon shooting pool. I was checking you out the whole time. Initially, you didn't notice me. You were in deep conversation. I told Miyanna *that you were going to be my man. So, I began ear hustling on your conversation with Greydon. You and Desirae had been arguing constantly. You felt like she wasn't making time for you, and your needs. You were starting to feel like she was more of a roommate rather, than your wife. There were many nights that you would come home from work, and you barely got a hug…kiss…let alone sex. That was my queue."*

"What do you mean?" I asked.

"Well, I knew I wanted to be with you. I just needed to figure out how I could make you mine. All I had to do was play my position - become the homegirl that you could confide and build your trust. Once you trusted me, I could get the inside scoop on the problems that you were having with your wife. From that night, we started communicating whenever she wasn't around you. She would go to bed after getting the kids settled for the night. You were still up. So, you would text me. We would spend hours flirting and sending pics back and forth. As time progressed, we started meeting at the park for lunch just to talk. Eventually, we would meet for a quickie."

I couldn't believe my ears. "So…you plotted to get me away from Desirae from the first moment that you saw me?"

"Well, I wouldn't say plotted. I saw what I wanted and went after it. And, we have been happily married for sixteen years."

She walked up behind me and hugged me. Jada had no idea that she had just added fuel to a fire that was already burning! I was extremely furious, but I didn't show it. As Jada put it, I played my position! But, I couldn't wait any longer.

"Now that I have finished cleaning, are you ready for your surprise?"

"Of course," she said with excitement.

"First, let me put this blindfold over your eyes."

"Ooohhh, this is going to be fun."

"Yep, it will be loads of fun! Give me your hand." I led her upstairs to our bedroom. "Are you ready?"

"Yes baby!" I took the blindfold off. "Wow, this is beautiful!"

There are red and white rose petals on the floor starting at the doorway leading to a heart shape on the bed. There were a dozen red roses in a white vase on Jada's side of the bed and a dozen white roses in a red vase on my side of the bed. There were also four different size gift boxes spaced out on the table near the bed.

"I see you put a lot of thought into this moment! Can I open the boxes?"

"Not yet. First, let me help you out of this dress."

I stood behind her and slipped my fingers through the spaghetti straps sliding one by one off her shoulders. I gently kissed the back of her neck. A low moan escaped her lips. Her dress dropped to the floor. I slipped my fingers through the loops on each side of her G-string. Then, I slid them down the curves of her body.

"Did you miss me?"

She whispered, "Yes, I missed you so much."

"Let me see."

I reached my hand in between her thighs.

"Mmmm…juicy! Yep, you're ready. Lay down on the bed."

I handcuffed her left wrist to the left post of the bed. I repeated the steps with her other wrist and both ankles.

"Ooohhh, we haven't used the handcuffs in a while."

"Yeah, I figured it was long overdue," I said.

After I made sure both wrists and ankles were secure, I stepped back and admired the view. Jada was looking at me with anticipation as I took my shirt off and unbuttoned my pants. I started unzipping my pants and then paused.

"Wait, I forgot something!"

"What?" she said sounding a bit irritated.

I walked over and stared in her eyes. Whack! I slapped her across the face so hard that the whole bed shook. A slight whimper escaped her mouth as a tear slid down her cheek.

"Why the fuck did you slap me? This is NOT a turn on!"

It's like a switch went off in my head! The loving husband that she once knew was gone. My facial expression displayed pure hate and evil.

"It's not meant to be BITCH!"

"Wait! Precious! Precious!"

"Oh, the safe word no longer applies," I said.

Fear covered her face because this was a side of me that she had never seen.

She cried, "Baby, why did you hit me?"

"Bitch, don't call me baby."

"Ba...Jayyson! You are scaring me! What is going on?"

"All this time? All this time, you have been playing me. Playing me for some weak nigga!"

"What are you talking about, Jayyson?" she asked as she squirmed.

"I turned my back on my family for you! I gave up my wife and kids for you! I trusted you with everything!"

Jada had a look of confusion written all over her face.

"You don't know what I'm talking about?"

"No, Jayyson! What are you talking about?" she asked.

"Jaxxson! Jerome!"

More tears escaped her eyes, but she asked, "What about them?"

"Bitch, don't play dumb! I had a long conversation with Jerome about all the trouble he has gotten into over the years. Trouble going back to when he was nine years old..."

Jada's tears were flowing like a river now.

"Jayyson!"

I hold my hand up and tell her, "Don't say anything! Jerome told us everything! He told me about all the times you were around him half-naked, bending over in front of him showing your ass, masturbating in front of him, showing him porn, and giving him weed and alcohol. Did I leave anything out?"

"Jayyson, you know that I would never do anything like that!"

"You raped my son for years!"

"No, that's not true! You know that I would never do anything like that, Jayyson!"

She squirmed even more, and I smacked her again.

"So, he's lying?"

"Yes."

"And, Jaxxson... I guess he was lying too?"

"Yes."

"Bitch, please!"

This time, I covered her mouth with the pink duct tape that was next to the boxes. Then, I lit a cigarette and took a few puffs. I began pacing back and forth.

"Jaxxson tried to tell me years ago, but I didn't believe him." I took another puff of the cigarette. "I haven't seen or spoken to Jaxxson or Charity in years! Justin and Jerome don't want anything to do with me!" I puffed again. "I turned my back on Desirae! And, to find out that you have been playing me from day one!" I puffed again. Jada started mumbling, so I snatched the tape off her mouth. She lets out a loud scream. "What? What do you have to say?"

"Jayyson, I am sorry!" she said.

"Oh, now you're sorry! A minute ago, they were lying! Which one is it?"

She was crying. I continued puffing the cigarette. "You did exactly what Jaxxson said you did, didn't you?"

She nodded in agreement.

"And, you did exactly what Jerome said you did, didn't you?"

She nodded her head again.

I punched her in the stomach. "Speak up!"

She gagged and moaned. "Yes, I did. Jaxxson and Jerome were telling the truth!"

"What about my cousin DoLo?"

"Yes, I did it!"

"And when Sonja saw you are the park with that guy, you were sleeping with him, weren't you?" I asked.

"Jayyson, please!"

I puffed the cigarette again. "Answer the question!"

"Yes. Jayyson, I promise I will never do anything like this again."

"Oh, I know you won't!" I said.

With her voice trembling, she said, "Jayyson, what are you going to do?"

Puffing on a cigarette, I replied, "I'm going to make sure that you never do anything like this to anyone ever again I put the butt out in the ashtray. "Oh, I almost forgot… your gifts! Do you want to see what I have for you?"

"No, I don't deserve any gifts," she said.

"These are special gifts. I picked each one with you in mind."

"I don't need any gifts, Jayyson," as tears streamed down her cheeks.

"Oh, yes you do! I bought these gifts specifically for you." I lit another cigarette. "Pick one… Box number one, two, three, or four?"

She just stared at me. I got ready to smack her again, and she quickly said, "Box number four!"

"Excellent choice! Let's open it! What do we have? A hunting knife!"

"What are you going to do with the knife?" she quivered.

I took a few puffs of the cigarette. "I'm so glad you asked. I remember when Jerome was nine years old… You had a bad habit of having him come sit by you. You would give him extra hugs and kisses on his cheeks. Jerome was hesitant, but he did what you asked. That's around the time when it started, huh?"

"No, please don't!" she said.

Puffing on a cigarette, I said, "There is no use begging. You deserve every bit of what you are about to get."

I took the knife and cut small slits on her thighs, legs, arms, stomach, feet, and face. Jada screamed and cried with each cut.

"Jayyson, I am sorry! Please stop!"

"We are just getting started!"

I cut more slits on her stomach, breasts, and face."

Screaming, she yelled, "Help! Somebody, please help me!"

I took the knife and jammed it into her arm.

Jada let out a loud scream while tears continued flowing down her face.

"You can scream all you want, but no one is coming. No one can hear you. Remember, that's why we bought this house… for seclusion. Now, shall we open another box?"

"No, please!" she begged.

"I really think that we should open another box. Pick one!"

"Box number one," she cried.

"Let's see what we have here… a semi-automatic pistol. Sorry, but it's not time for this gift yet."

I took a few puffs from my cigarette. Jada cried louder and louder.

"Shut up, Jada! Ain't that what you used to say to Jaxxson… Shut up, Jaxxson? Oh, and Jerome. Shut up, Jerome!" I said.

"Please Jayyson!"

"Pick another box."

I took a few more puffs of my cigarette and put the butt out in the ashtray.

"Box number three," she cried.

"A nice wooden bat. I remember when Jerome was eleven years old… You asked me to start calling you before I came home from work. You said you wanted to make sure my dinner was warmed and ready when I got home. So, you thought it was ok to steal the innocence of children?"

Whack! I hit her on her left knee cap. She screamed out in pain.

"Jayyson, please stop! I am so sorry! You made your point! I will never do it again!"

"No, I don't think so!"

I put the tape back over her mouth. Whack! I hit her right kneecap. I heard a loud cracking noise.

Laughing, I said, "Sounds like a broken knee cap. I know that shit hurt!" Whack! I hit her left kneecap again. I hear another loud cracking noise." Laughing, I said, "Two for two!"

She mumbled in pain.

"You thought it was okay to fuck little boys?"
She mumbled while shaking her head no.

"Yes, you did! You thought it was ok. You continued to do it for years!"

I used the top part of the bat and jammed it into her stomach. She let out a muffled groan.

"Let's open the last box. Box number two. My favorite… an electric branding iron."

I plugged the branding iron into the outlet by the bed.

"I'm sure you're wondering why I selected the branding iron. I remember when Jerome was thirteen years old… There were a couple times that I forgot to call before I headed home. I walked in the door and said "Baby, I'm home." Then, I heard a loud commotion upstairs. I rushed upstairs and saw you on the floor naked, sweating, and out of breath. You said, 'I was about to get in the shower before you got home. Baby, I just fell. My leg gave out again. I tried to get up but obviously that didn't work.' I said, 'You really need to get that checked. Seems like it's happening more and more.' Then, you asked, 'Why didn't you call?' I said, 'I didn't think about it. It's been a rough day. I just wanted to get home. Where is Jerome?' I asked. You said he was in his room. He appeared in the hallway. I asked him why his boxers were on backwards. He said he was about to get in the shower, but he heard me call him. So, you had just got through fucking my son, didn't you?"

I picked up the hot branding iron and hovered it over to her skin. Jada's muffled screams got louder.

"As I recall, that's when you wanted to put the tracker on my phone. Safety was your reason. Safety my ass! You just wanted to make sure I didn't interrupt you! Hhhmmm... Do I want to start with fingers, toes, breasts, or pussy?"

I hovered the branding iron over each option. More muffled cries.

"Pussy it is!"

I laid the branding iron on her freshly waxed pussy. I heard the sizzling of her burning flesh.

"Crying is not going to help you! You didn't care when my boys cried, did you?"

I removed the branding iron from her burning flesh. Then, I snatched the tape from her mouth.

"You damaged Jaxxson and Jerome! What kind of person does that shit to children? What the fuck is wrong with you?"

I placed the branding iron briefly on her left breast and then the right breast. She let out blood curdling scream.

"Jayyson, stop! You have made your point! You don't have to do this! You can let me go, and I could just disappear from your life forever!" she said.

"Nah, that would be way too easy. You wouldn't do anything but wait until a little time has passed and go back to doing the same thing to someone else's child."

I stopped and lit another cigarette and took a few puffs. Then, I grabbed the gun off the table and asked, "Do you have any last words?"

"I'm sorry, Jayyson! I never meant to hurt anyone. My dad… My dad started abusing me when I was ten years old. That was right after my mom passed away. After Mama passed away, Daddy spent a lot of time drinking. He was angry at Mama for leaving him. He used to take his anger out on me. At first, it was a slap here and a punch there. As I got older, I got hips and breasts. I already looked like my Mama, but now I had the body like her.

"Daddy had been drinking all day. I tried my best to stay out of his way. I went all day without crossing his path until I took off my clothes because I was about to get in the shower. I forgot to lock the door. He came bursting into the bathroom. This time, there was a different look on his face. He started searching my body with his eyes. I reach for my bathrobe to cover up. He told me I looked just like my mama. I told him I knew that. Then, he came over and grabbed my wrist. He dragged me out of the bathroom and took me to his bedroom. Porn was playing on the TV. 'No, daddy!' I yelled and tried to pry his grip from my wrist, but I fell.

"He slapped me across my face and said, 'Come here, I'm going to teach you how to keep a man.' I tried to get away and said, 'No, daddy!' He slapped me so hard that I fell to the ground. Then, he unzipped his pants and sat in his chair. He pulled his dick out and said, 'Jada, get on your knees facing me.' Crying, I said, 'Daddy, I don't want to do this!' He slapped my face again. 'Shut up! I own you! You do as I say!' Daddy made me suck his dick! I was thirteen years old. At first, that's all that I had to do, and he would go straight to sleep. But, he spent more and more time staring at Mama's picture. He made me watch porn to learn how to please him sexually. Eventually, he started making me have sex with him. That continued until I was eighteen years old. That's when I left home and never went back

"I did try telling Aunt Sweet when it started, but she slapped me! She said, 'You should be ashamed for lying on your father like that! He is a God-fearing man!' In her eyes, he wouldn't do anything like that because he was a deacon in the church. No one helped me! After that, I never attempted to tell anyone else. If I could go back in time, I would have told until someone believed me," she cried.

"So, you know what it's like to be abused. Yet, you turn around and do that shit to someone else? My boys! I am truly sorry that you were abused... but... that doesn't change what you did to my boys!"

Pow! I shot Jada right between her eyes!

"That was for Jaxxson and Jerome!"

I just sat there and stared at her for what seemed like an eternity. I spent hours contemplating whether or not I should commit suicide. Finally, I placed the barrel of the gun to my forehead and pulled the trigger, but it jammed. So, I figured it wasn't time for me to die yet. That's when I called Greydon.

"Hey bro!" I said.

"Whassup?"

"She hurt them! It happened right under my nose for years and I couldn't see it!"

"Jayyson, what are you talking about? What happened right under your nose?" he asked.

"Jada hurt Jaxxson and Jerome. Jaxxson tried to tell me years ago, but I wouldn't listen!"

"What happened, Jayyson?"

Crying, I said, *"Jerome told me a couple of days ago what led him to a life of a crime. Jada had been abusing him since he was nine years old. Nine, bruh! This bitch has been raping my boy for years!"*

"Jayyson, where is Jada?"

Silence.

"Jayyson, what did you do?" he asked.

Silence.

"Jayyson!"

I finally said, "Yeah, I'm here."

"Where are you?"

"I'm at home."

"Where is Jada?"

"She's right here."

"I know you, man! What did you do to Jada?" he asked.

"Call the police."

"Why? What did you do to Jada?"

"I killed her," I confessed.

"Oh shit! Baby, let me see your phone."

I heard him dial 9-1-1.

"9-1-1, what's your emergency?" the operator said.

"Send the police to 5150 Synn Circle. My friend is on the other line. He killed his wife."

"What's the friend's name?"

"Jayyson Craig."

"What is your name, sir?"

"*Greydon James.*"

"*Officers are in route to 5150 Synn Circle,*" she said.

Greydon hung up the phone before the operator could ask anything else.

"*Jayyson? Are you still there?*"

"*Yeah, man. I'm here,*" I cried.

"*The police are on the way.*"

"*Greydon, can you do me a favor?*"

"*Anything!*"

"*I wrote a letter to my kids before I killed Jada. I put the letters in an envelope and mailed them to you. Can you make sure they get them?*"

"*Consider it done!*"

I heard sirens outside my house. "*I'm sorry that I allowed Jada to jeopardize my relationship with you. I love you, man!*"

"*I love you, too!*"

Then, I heard a loud voice. "*This is Lieutenant Jamison. Jayyson Craig. Come out with your hands up.*"

I surrendered, and they took me away without a fight.

My attorney stopped recording and stared at me in disbelief. They had their confession.

Voice of Tears

About the Author

Christian S. Branch hails from Little Rock, Arkansas. She's a mother of two and an active member in her church.

When she's not spending time with family, she's writing her latest best seller. Christian will earn her Bachelor of Business Administration in Management from the University of Arkansas in the Fall 2023.

To keep up with her latest works, follow her at www.amazon.com/author/ChristianSBranch.

www.ingramcontent.com/pod-product-compliance
Lightning Source LLC
Chambersburg PA
CBHW051513260626
47162CB00008B/2949